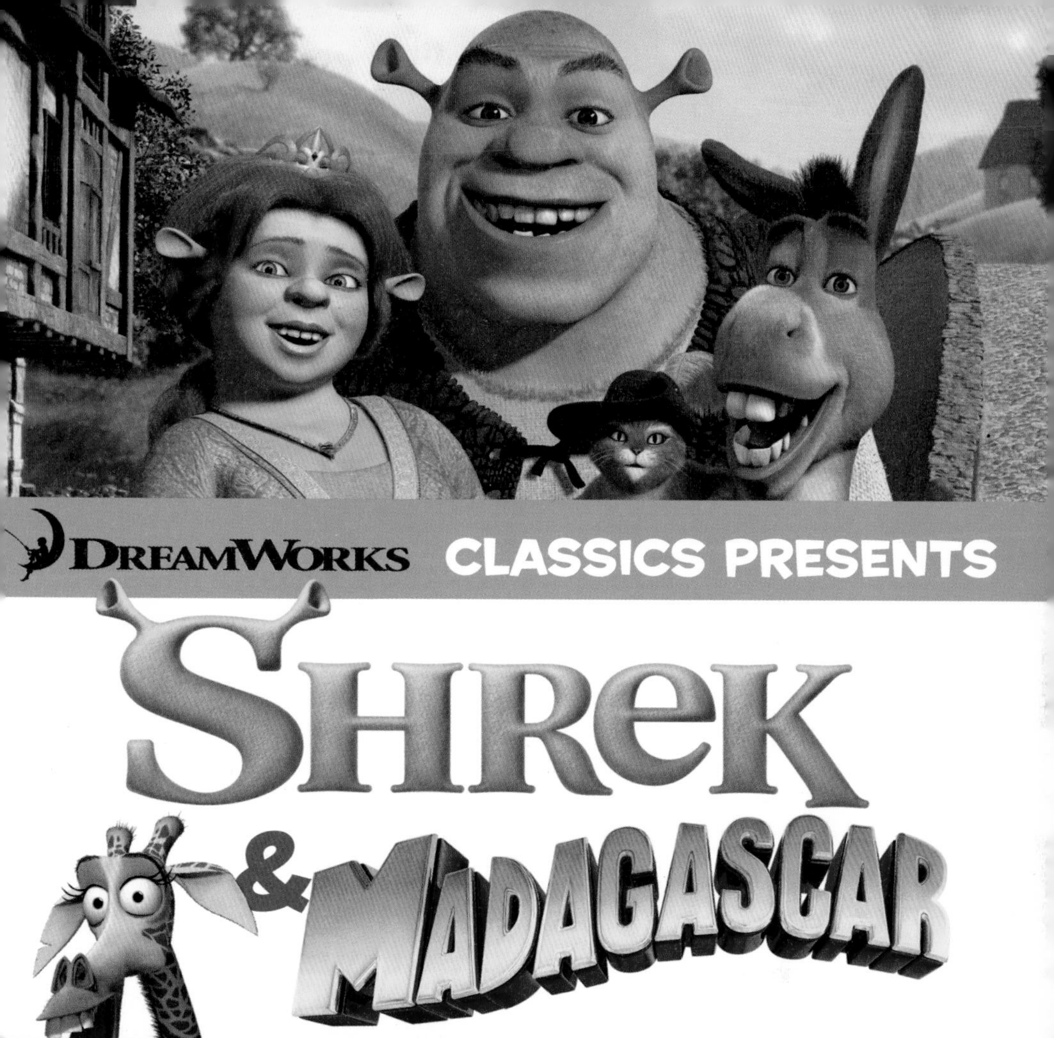

DreamWorks Classics Presents

Shrek & Madagascar

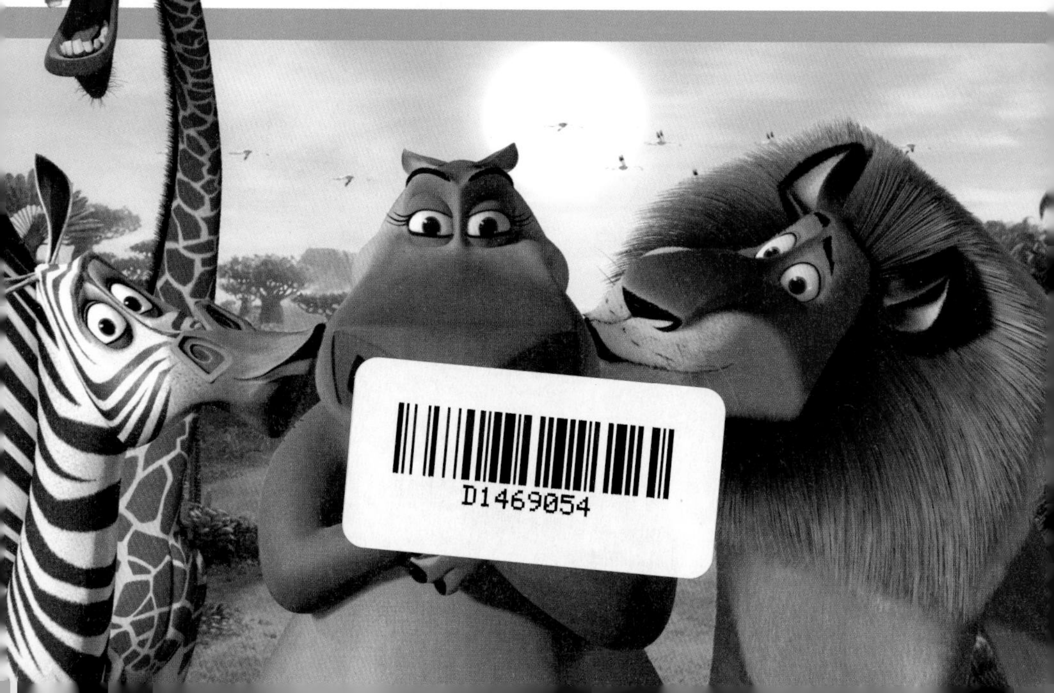

CONTENTS

SHREK COMICS!

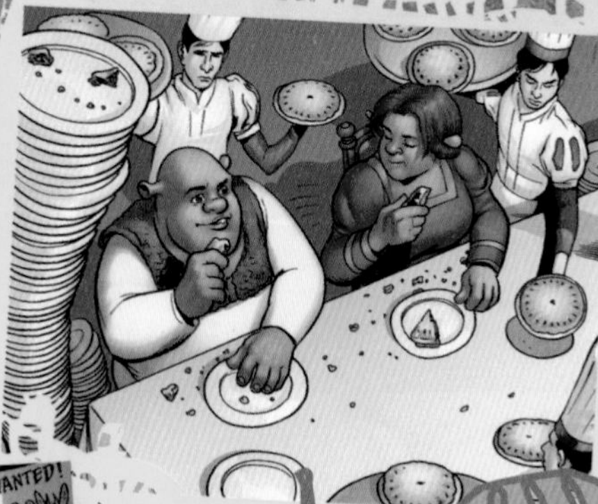

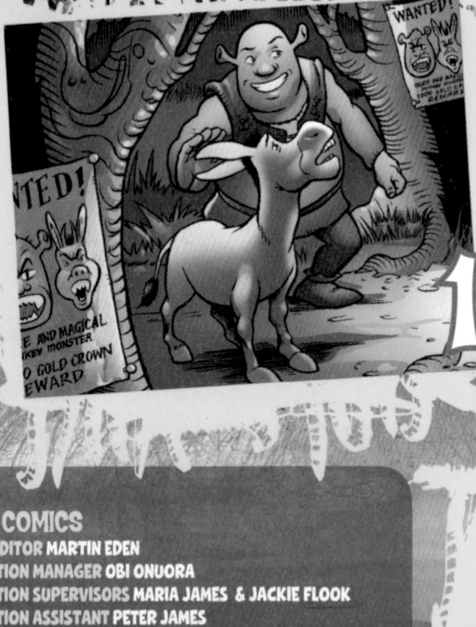
WANTED!

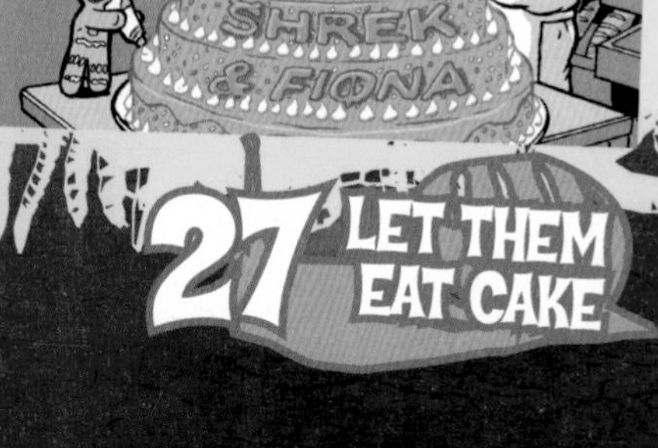
HAPPY ANNIVERSARY SHREK & FIONA

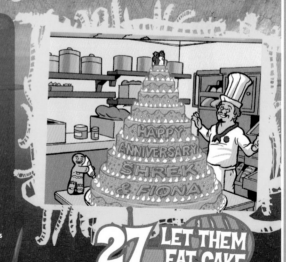

TITAN COMICS
SENIOR EDITOR MARTIN EDEN
PRODUCTION MANAGER OBI ONUORA
PRODUCTION SUPERVISORS MARIA JAMES & JACKIE FLOOK
PRODUCTION ASSISTANT PETER JAMES
ART DIRECTOR OZ BROWNE
SENIOR SALES MANAGER STEVE TOTHILL
DIRECT SALES & MARKETING MANAGER RICKY CLAYDON
PUBLISHING MANAGER DARRYL TOTHILL
PUBLISHING DIRECTOR CHRIS TEATHER
OPERATIONS DIRECTOR LEIGH BAULCH
EXECUTIVE DIRECTOR VIVIAN CHEUNG
PUBLISHER NICK LANDAU

DreamWorks Classics Volume Four: Let Them Eat Cake
ISBN: 9781782762492
Published by Titan Comics,
a division of Titan Publishing Group Ltd.
144 Southwark St. London, SE1 0UP

10 9 8 7 6 5 4 3 2 1
First printed in China in December 2016.
A CIP catalogue record for this title is available from the British Library.

DreamWorks CLASSICS PRESENTS

SHREK & MADAGASCAR

MADAGASCAR STORIES!

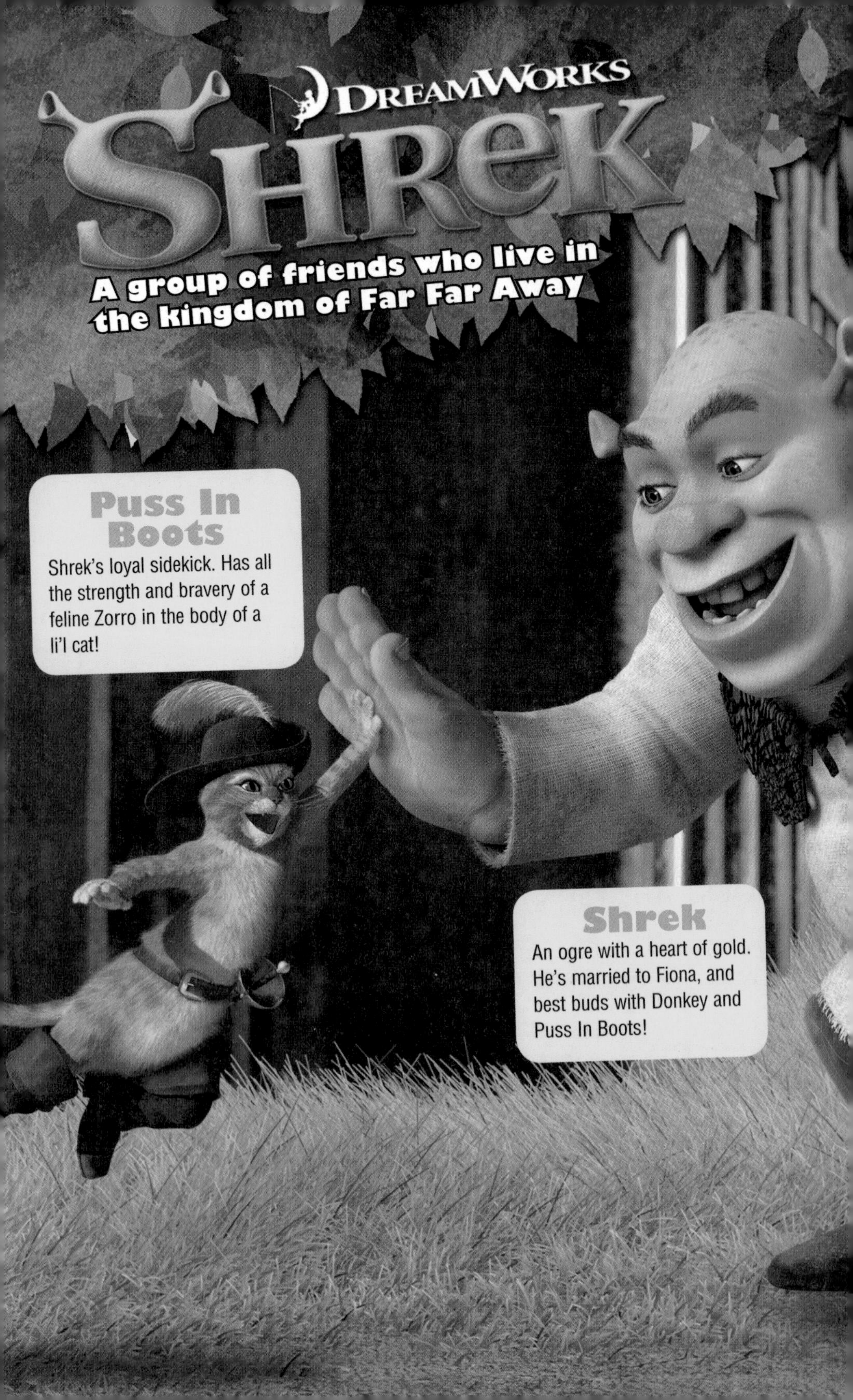
DreamWorks

Shrek

A group of friends who live in the kingdom of Far Far Away

Puss In Boots

Shrek's loyal sidekick. Has all the strength and bravery of a feline Zorro in the body of a li'l cat!

Shrek

An ogre with a heart of gold. He's married to Fiona, and best buds with Donkey and Puss In Boots!

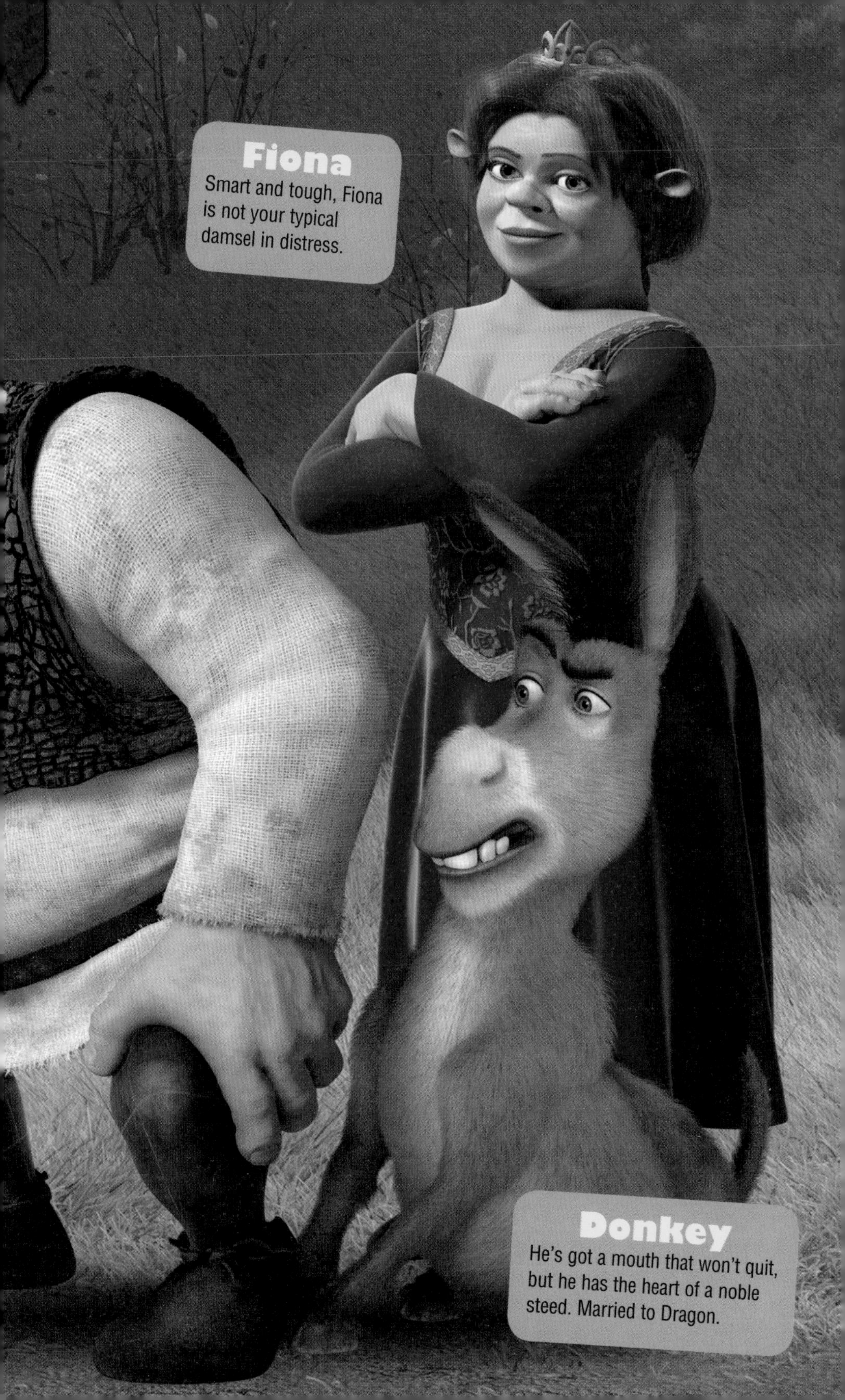
Fiona
Smart and tough, Fiona is not your typical damsel in distress.
Donkey
He's got a mouth that won't quit, but he has the heart of a noble steed. Married to Dragon.

THE PIEMAN COMETH

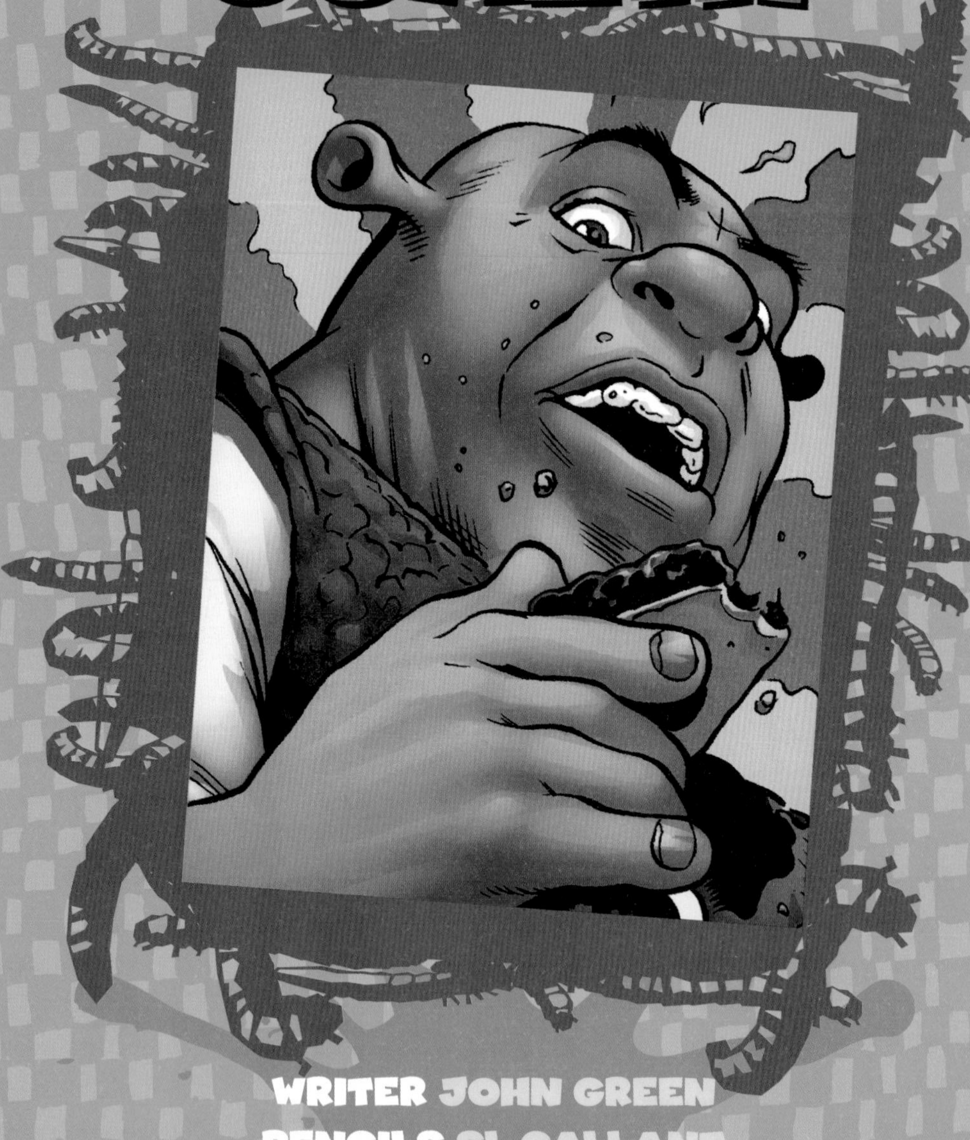

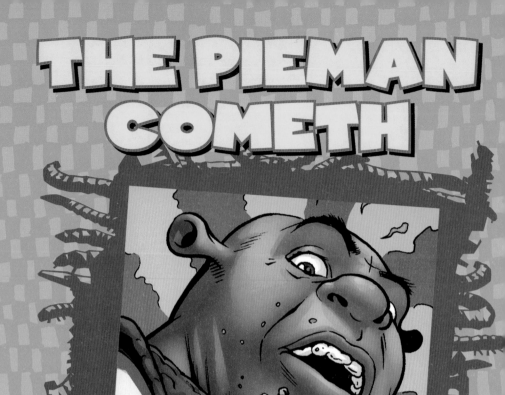

WRITER JOHN GREEN
PENCILS SL GALLANT
INKS GARY ERSKINE
COLORS HI-FI DESIGN
LETTERS JIMMY BETANCOURT/COMICRAFT

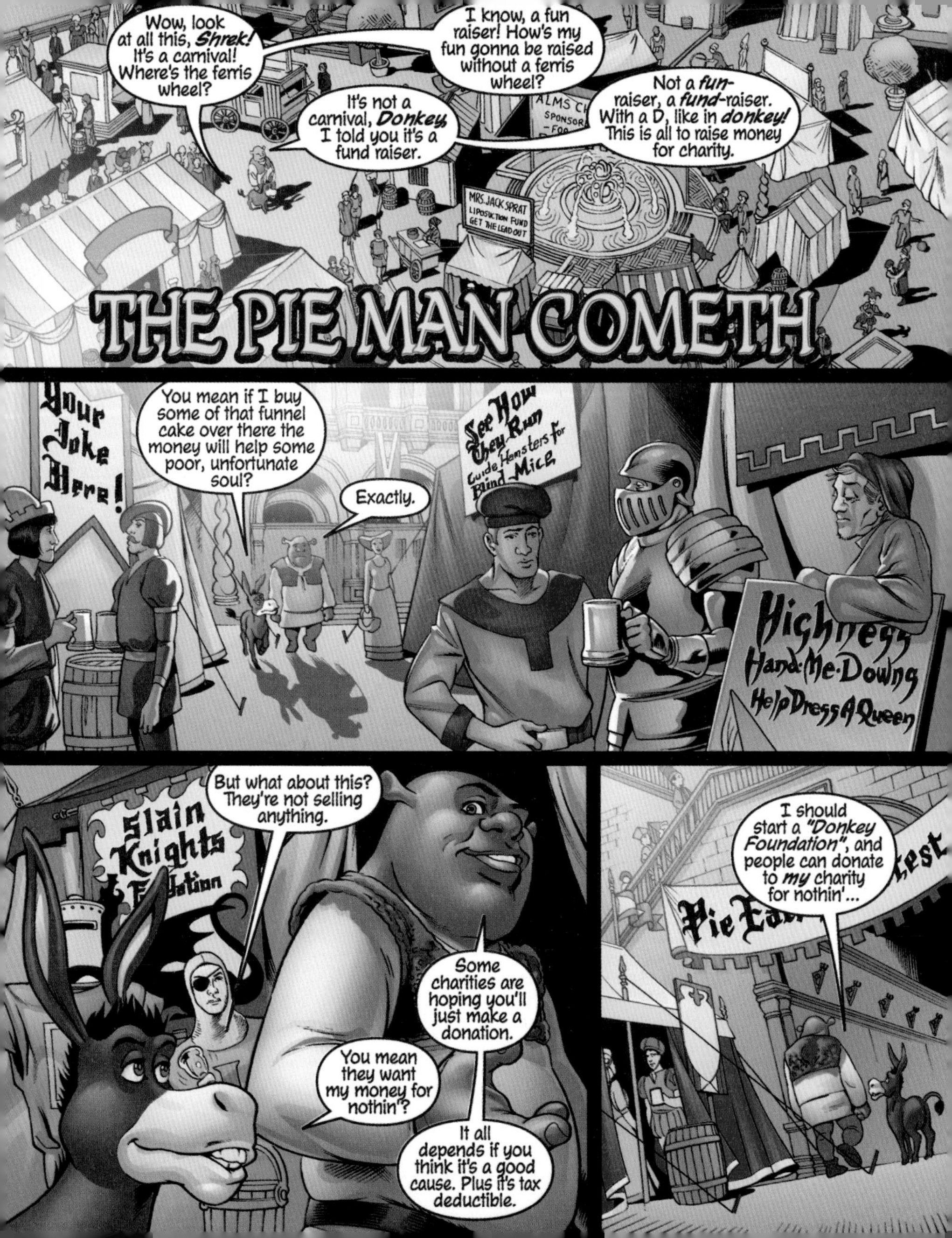
Wow, look at all this, Shrek! It's a carnival! Where's the ferris wheel?
It's not a carnival, Donkey. I told you it's a fund raiser.
I know, a fun raiser! How's my fun gonna be raised without a ferris wheel?
Not a fun-raiser, a fund-raiser. With a D, like in donkey! This is all to raise money for charity.
MRS. JACK SPRAT LIPOSUCTION FUND GET THE LEAD OUT
THE PIE MAN COMETH
Your Joke Here!
You mean if I buy some of that funnel cake over there the money will help some poor, unfortunate soul?
Exactly.
See How They Run Guide Hamsters for Blind Mice
Highness Hand-Me-Downs Help Dress A Queen
Slain Knights
But what about this? They're not selling anything.
Some charities are hoping you'll just make a donation.
You mean they want my money for nothin'?
It all depends if you think it's a good cause. Plus it's tax deductible.
I should start a "Donkey Foundation", and people can donate to my charity for nothin'...

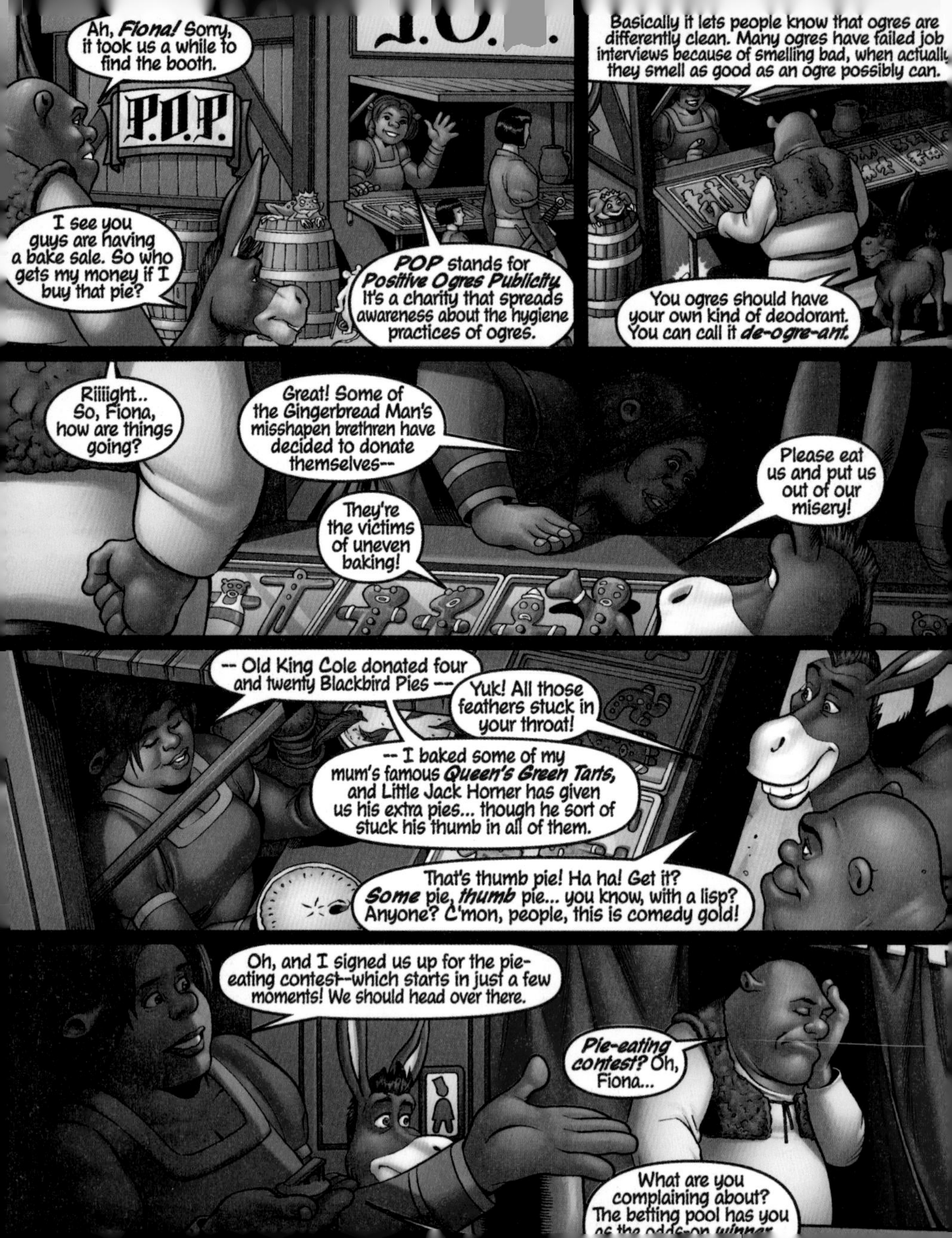
Ah, Fiona! Sorry, it took us a while to find the booth.
P.O.P.
I see you guys are having a bake sale. So who gets my money if I buy that pie?
POP stands for Positive Ogres Publicity. It's a charity that spreads awareness about the hygiene practices of ogres.
Basically it lets people know that ogres are differently clean. Many ogres have failed job interviews because of smelling bad, when actually they smell as good as an ogre possibly can.
You ogres should have your own kind of deodorant. You can call it de-ogre-ant.
Riiiight.. So, Fiona, how are things going?
Great! Some of the Gingerbread Man's misshapen brethren have decided to donate themselves--
They're the victims of uneven baking!
Please eat us and put us out of our misery!
-- Old King Cole donated four and twenty Blackbird Pies --
Yuk! All those feathers stuck in your throat!
-- I baked some of my mum's famous Queen's Green Tarts, and Little Jack Horner has given us his extra pies... though he sort of stuck his thumb in all of them.
That's thumb pie! Ha ha! Get it? Some pie, thumb pie... you know, with a lisp? Anyone? C'mon, people, this is comedy gold!
Oh, and I signed us up for the pie-eating contest--which starts in just a few moments! We should head over there.
Pie-eating contest? Oh, Fiona...
What are you complaining about? The betting pool has you

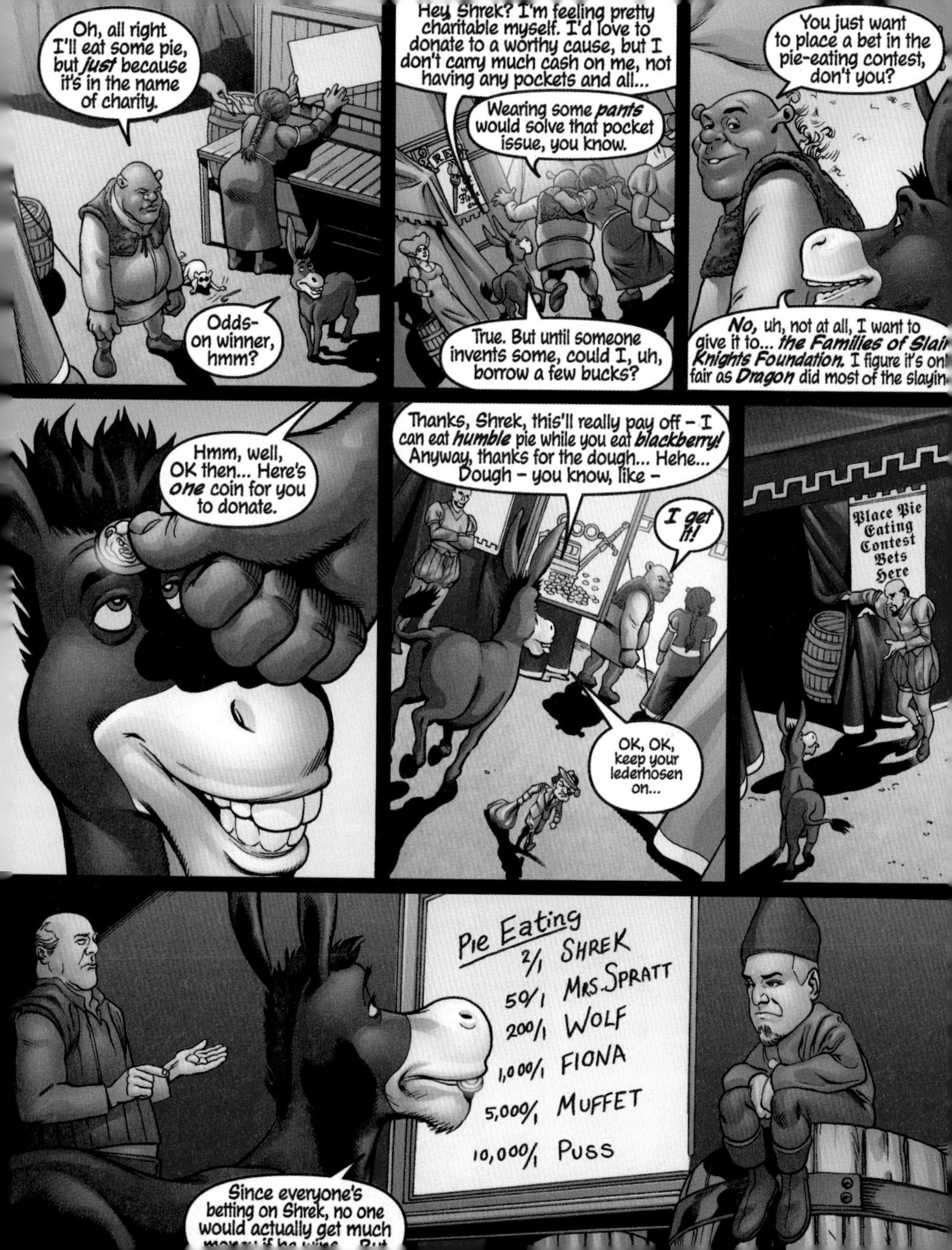

Oh, all right I'll eat some pie, but *just* because it's in the name of charity.
Odds-on winner, hmm?
Hey Shrek? I'm feeling pretty charitable myself. I'd love to donate to a worthy cause, but I don't carry much cash on me, not having any pockets and all...
Wearing some *pants* would solve that pocket issue, you know.
True. But until someone invents some, could I, uh, borrow a few bucks?
You just want to place a bet in the pie-eating contest, don't you?
No, uh, not at all, I want to give it to... *the Families of Slai Knights Foundation.* I figure it's onl fair as *Dragon* did most of the slayin
Hmm, well, OK then... Here's *one* coin for you to donate.
Thanks, Shrek, this'll really pay off – I can eat *humble* pie while you eat *blackberry!* Anyway, thanks for the dough... Hehe... Dough – you know, like –
I get it!
OK, OK, keep your lederhosen on...
Place Pie Eating Contest Bets Here
Pie Eating
2/1 SHREK
50/1 MRS.SPRATT
200/1 WOLF
1,000/1 FIONA
5,000/1 MUFFET
10,000/1 PUSS
Since everyone's betting on Shrek, no one would actually get much

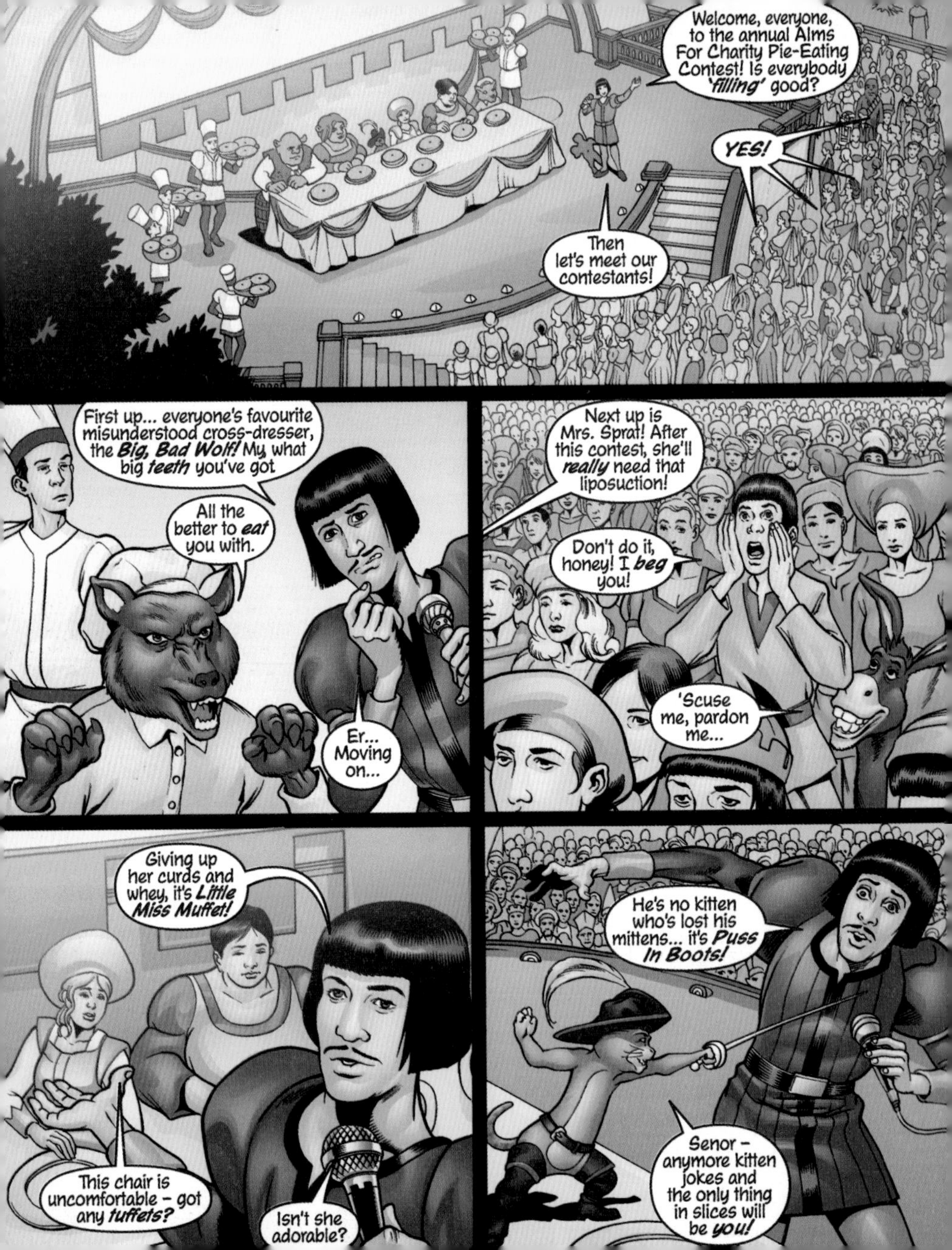

Welcome, everyone, to the annual Alms For Charity Pie-Eating Contest! Is everybody *'filling'* good?
YES!
Then let's meet our contestants!
First up... everyone's favourite misunderstood cross-dresser, the ***Big, Bad Wolf!*** My, what big ***teeth*** you've got
All the better to ***eat*** you with.
Er... Moving on...
Next up is Mrs. Sprat! After this contest, she'll ***really*** need that liposuction!
Don't do it, honey! I ***beg*** you!
'Scuse me, pardon me...
Giving up her curds and whey, it's ***Little Miss Muffet!***
This chair is uncomfortable – got any ***tuffets?***
Isn't she adorable?
He's no kitten who's lost his mittens... it's ***Puss In Boots!***
Senor – anymore kitten jokes and the only thing in slices will be ***you!***

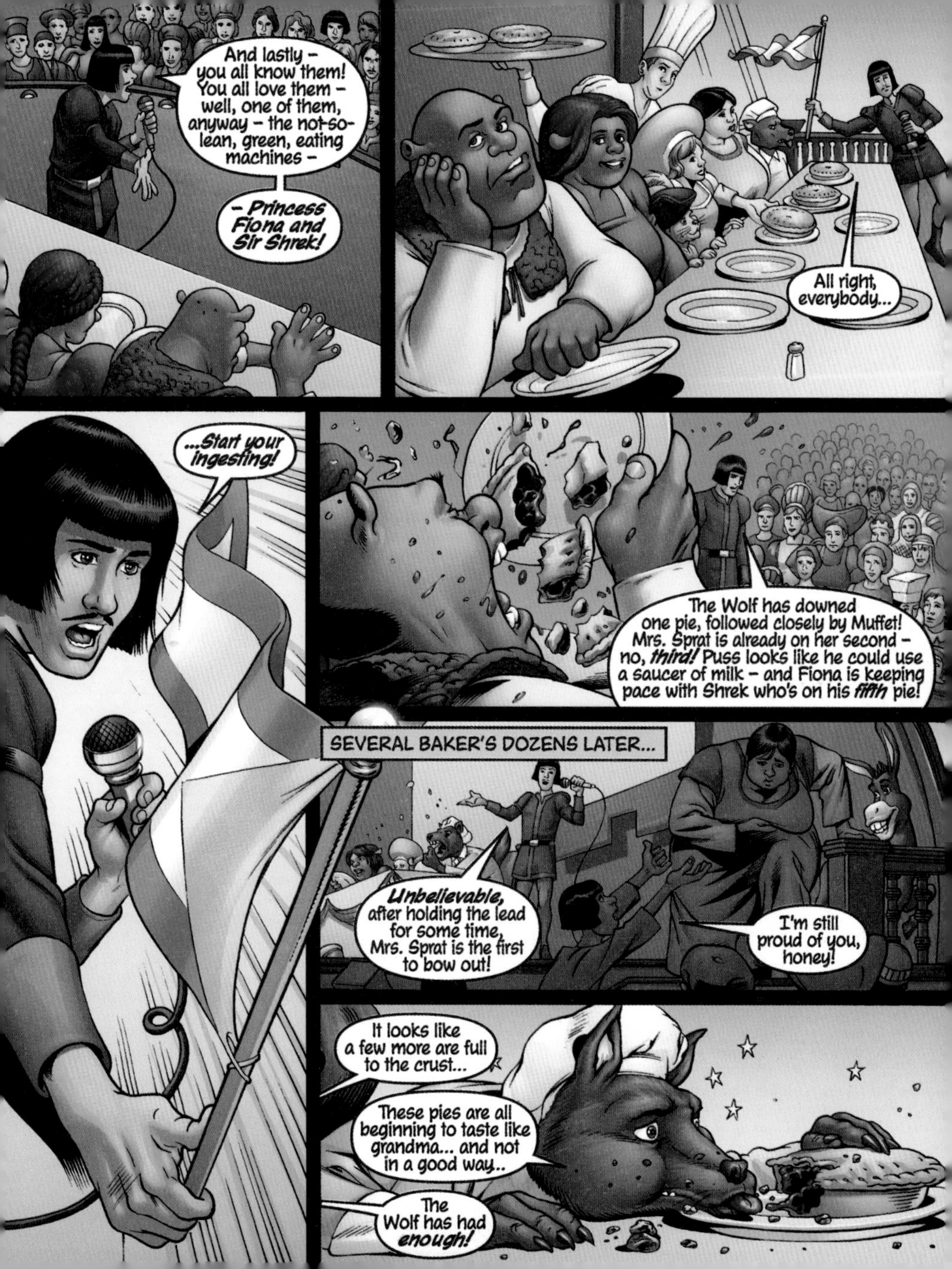

And lastly – you all know them! You all love them – well, one of them, anyway – the not-so-lean, green, eating machines –
– Princess Fiona and Sir Shrek!
All right, everybody...
...Start your ingesting!
The Wolf has downed one pie, followed closely by Muffet! Mrs. Sprat is already on her second – no, third! Puss looks like he could use a saucer of milk – and Fiona is keeping pace with Shrek who's on his fifth pie!
SEVERAL BAKER'S DOZENS LATER...
Unbelievable, after holding the lead for some time, Mrs. Sprat is the first to bow out!
I'm still proud of you, honey!
It looks like a few more are full to the crust...
These pies are all beginning to taste like grandma... and not in a good way..
The Wolf has had enough!

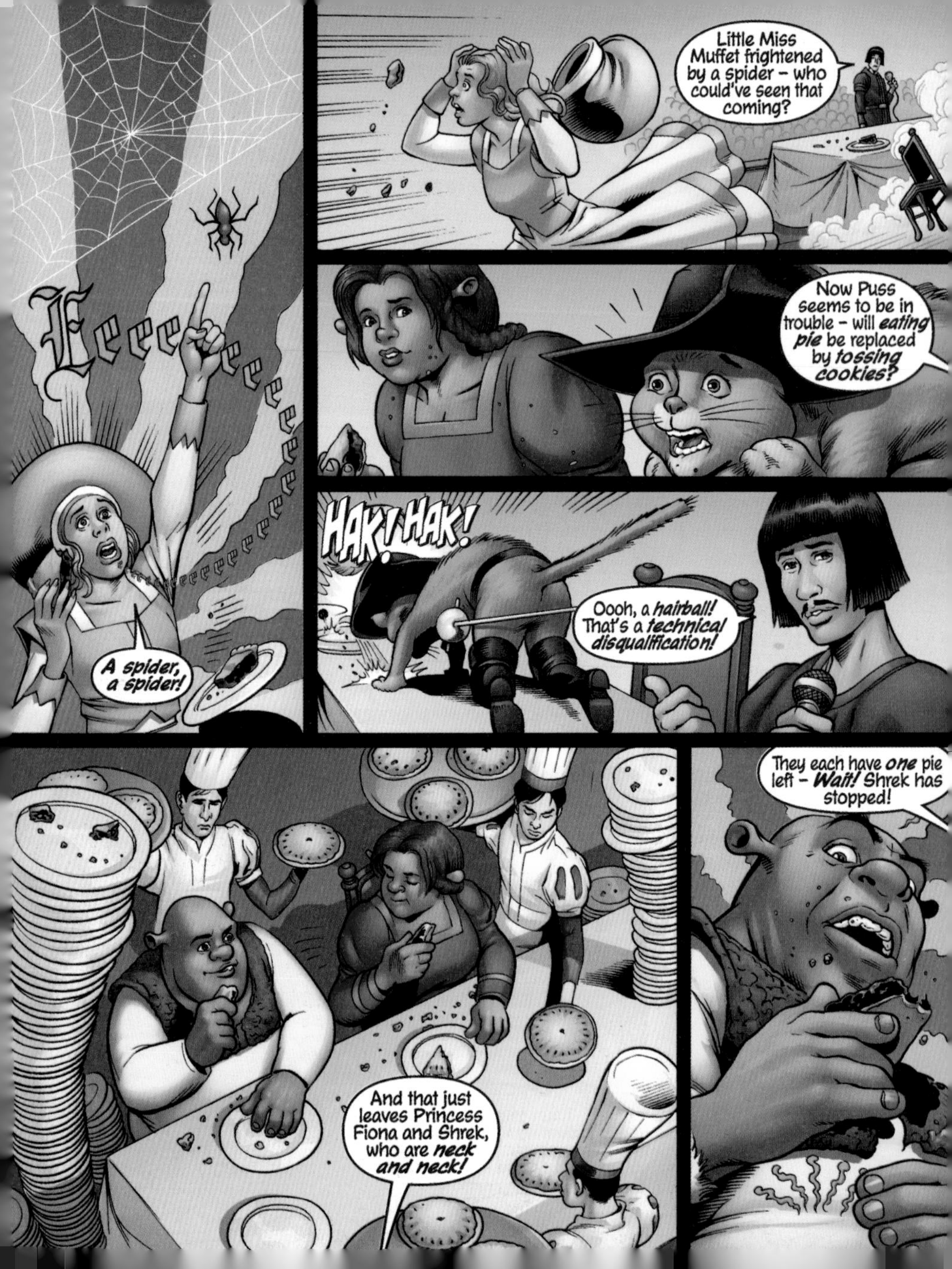

Eeeeeeeeeeeeeeeeeeeeeeeeeeee
A spider, a spider!
Little Miss Muffet frightened by a spider – who could've seen that coming?
Now Puss seems to be in trouble – will eating pie be replaced by tossing cookies?
HAK! HAK!
Oooh, a hairball! That's a technical disqualification!
And that just leaves Princess Fiona and Shrek, who are neck and neck!
They each have one pie left – Wait! Shrek has stopped!

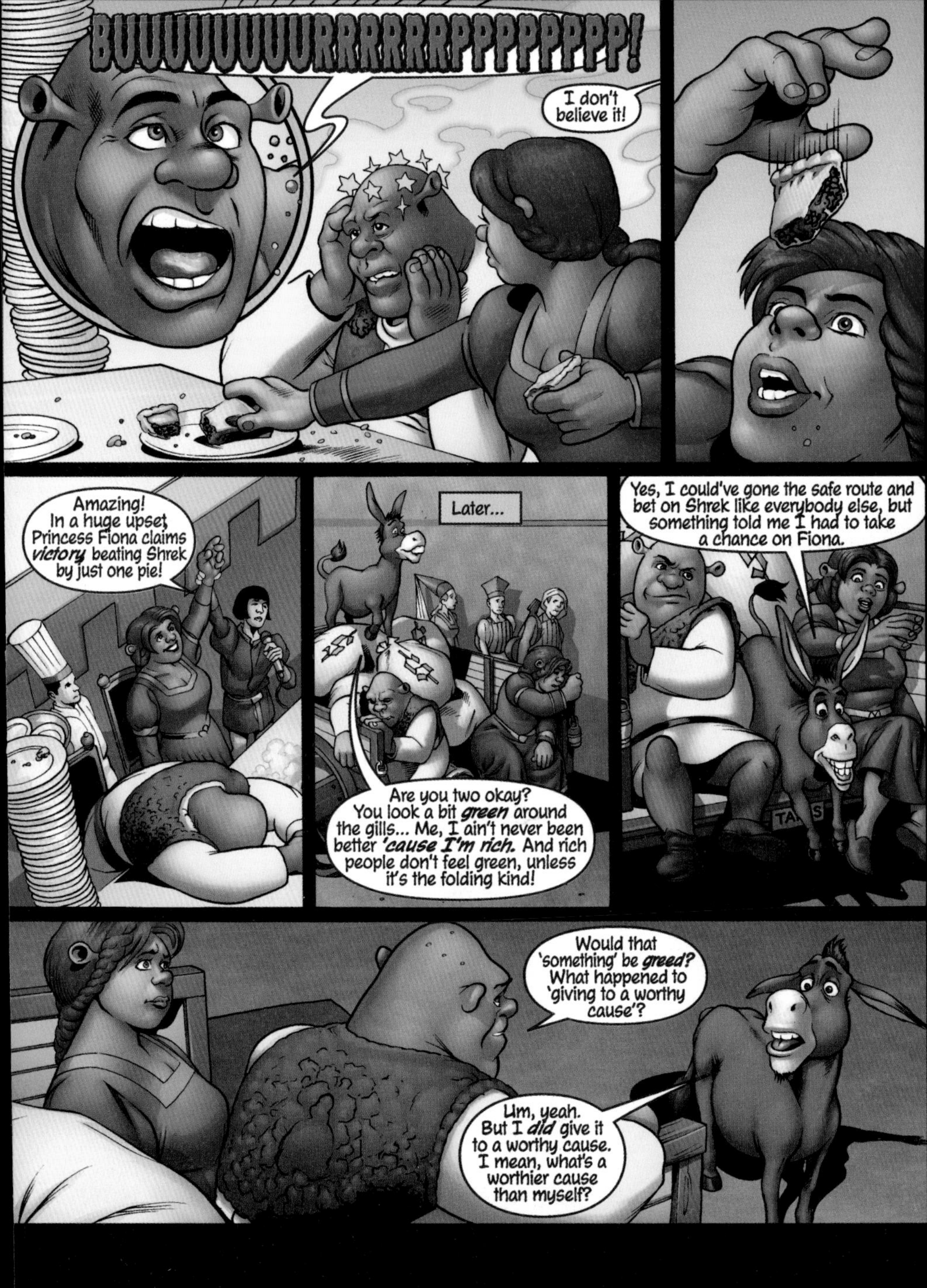
BUUUUUUUURRRRRRPPPPPPPP!
I don't believe it!
Amazing! In a huge upset, Princess Fiona claims victory beating Shrek by just one pie!
Later...
Are you two okay? You look a bit green around the gills... Me, I ain't never been better 'cause I'm rich. And rich people don't feel green, unless it's the folding kind!
Yes, I could've gone the safe route and bet on Shrek like everybody else, but something told me I had to take a chance on Fiona.
Would that 'something' be greed? What happened to 'giving to a worthy cause'?
Um, yeah. But I did give it to a worthy cause. I mean, what's a worthier cause than myself?

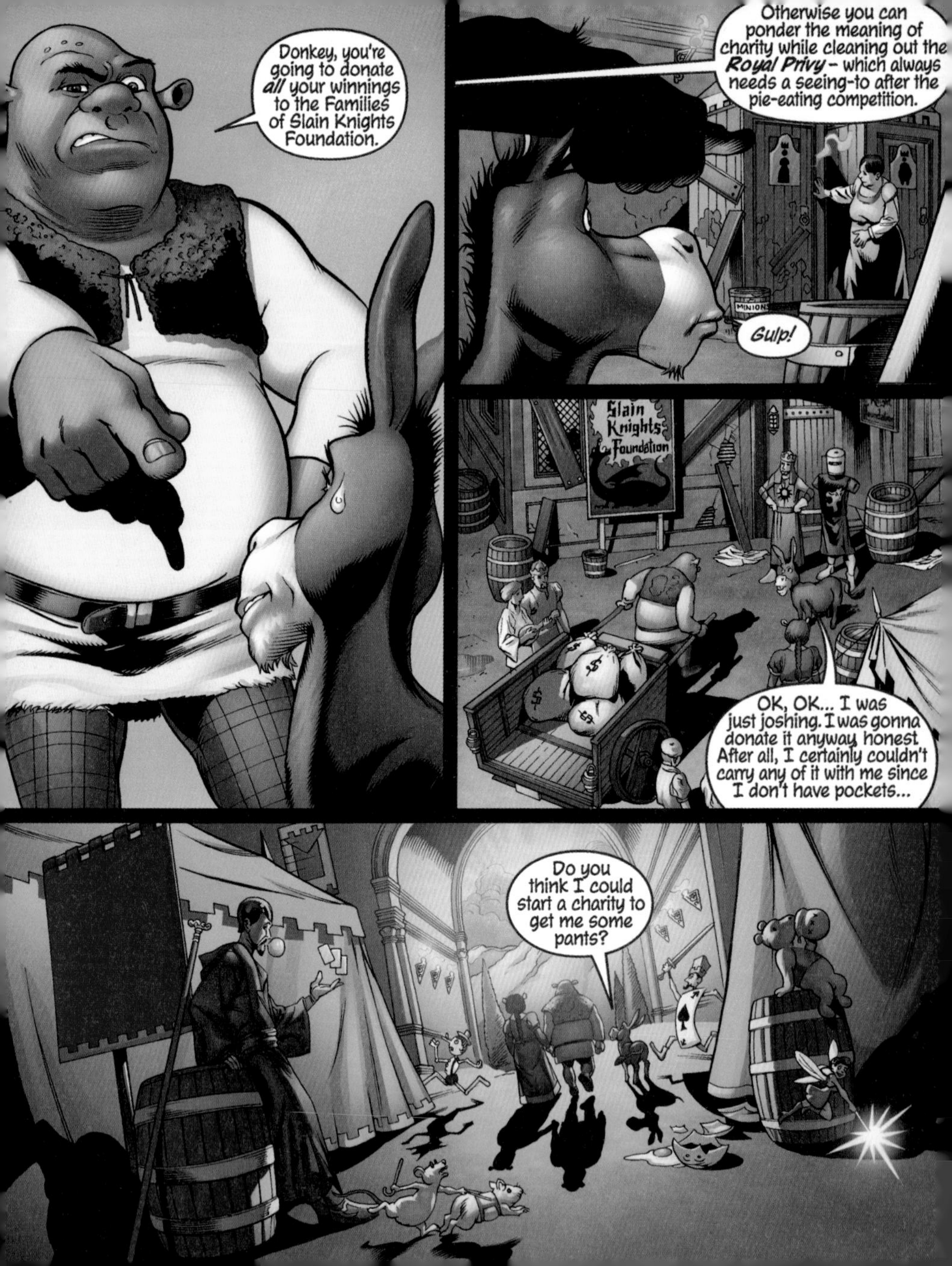

Donkey, you're going to donate all your winnings to the Families of Slain Knights Foundation.
Otherwise you can ponder the meaning of charity while cleaning out the Royal Privy – which always needs a seeing-to after the pie-eating competition.
MINIONS
Gulp!
Slain Knights Foundation
OK, OK... I was just joshing. I was gonna donate it anyway honest After all, I certainly couldn't carry any of it with me since I don't have pockets...
Do you think I could start a charity to get me some pants?

THE BLACK KNIGHT

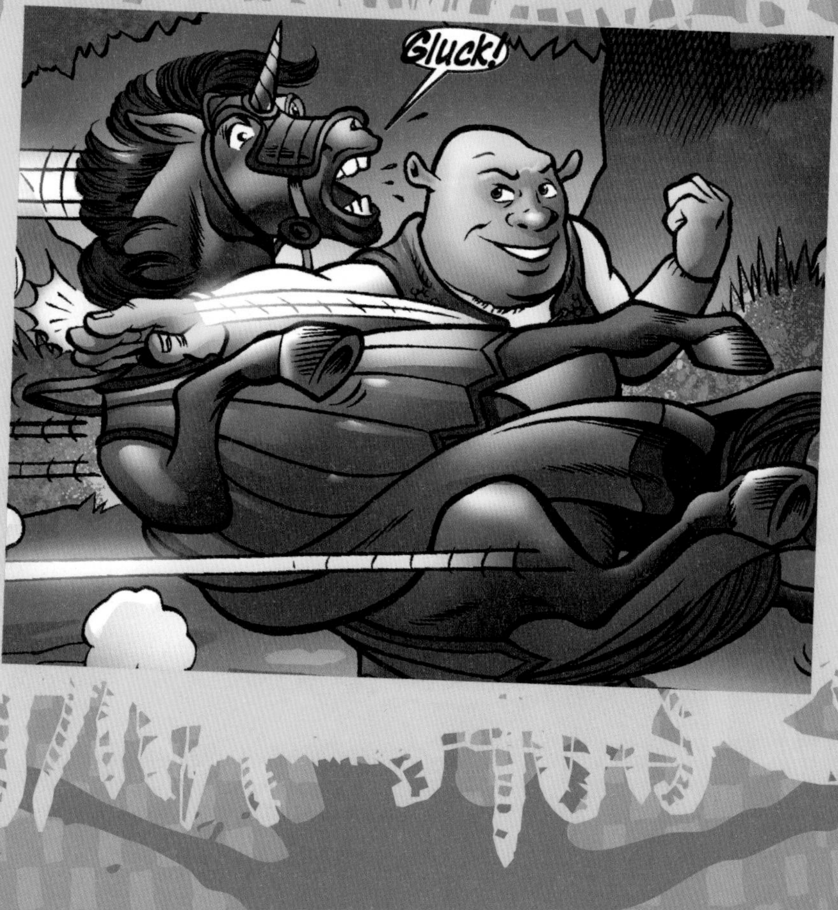
GLUCK!

WRITER JAI NITZ
PENCIL BRIAN WILLIAMSON
INKS BAMBOS GEORGIOU
COLORS DAN KEMP
LETTERS JIMMY BETANCOURT/COMICRAFT

Gather 'round, lads, and I'll tell ya a tale of Grant Gravestone, the Black Knight of the Black Forest!

Grant Gravestone! He fought the bridge troll of Banaack Baeren!

Aye, and he slew the white dragon, Silver Wyrm.

But he once fought villain so fou so evil, so malodorous he could onl be called...

THE BLACK KNIGHT

Shrek!

You seen this?

It's a wanted poster, Donkey. There's always a new one posted by some villainous type with an axe to grind. As an ogre, you get used to it.

Maybe you get used to it, but this is the first time I've been a wanted donkey. I don't want no one grinding no axe on me! What are we gonna do? Go on the lam?

Nonsense. No one ever looks at those, Donkey.

WANTED!

OGRE AND MAGICAL DONKEY MONSTER
1000 GOLD CROWN REWARD

WANTED

OGRE AND MA DONKEY MON 1000 GOLD REWARD

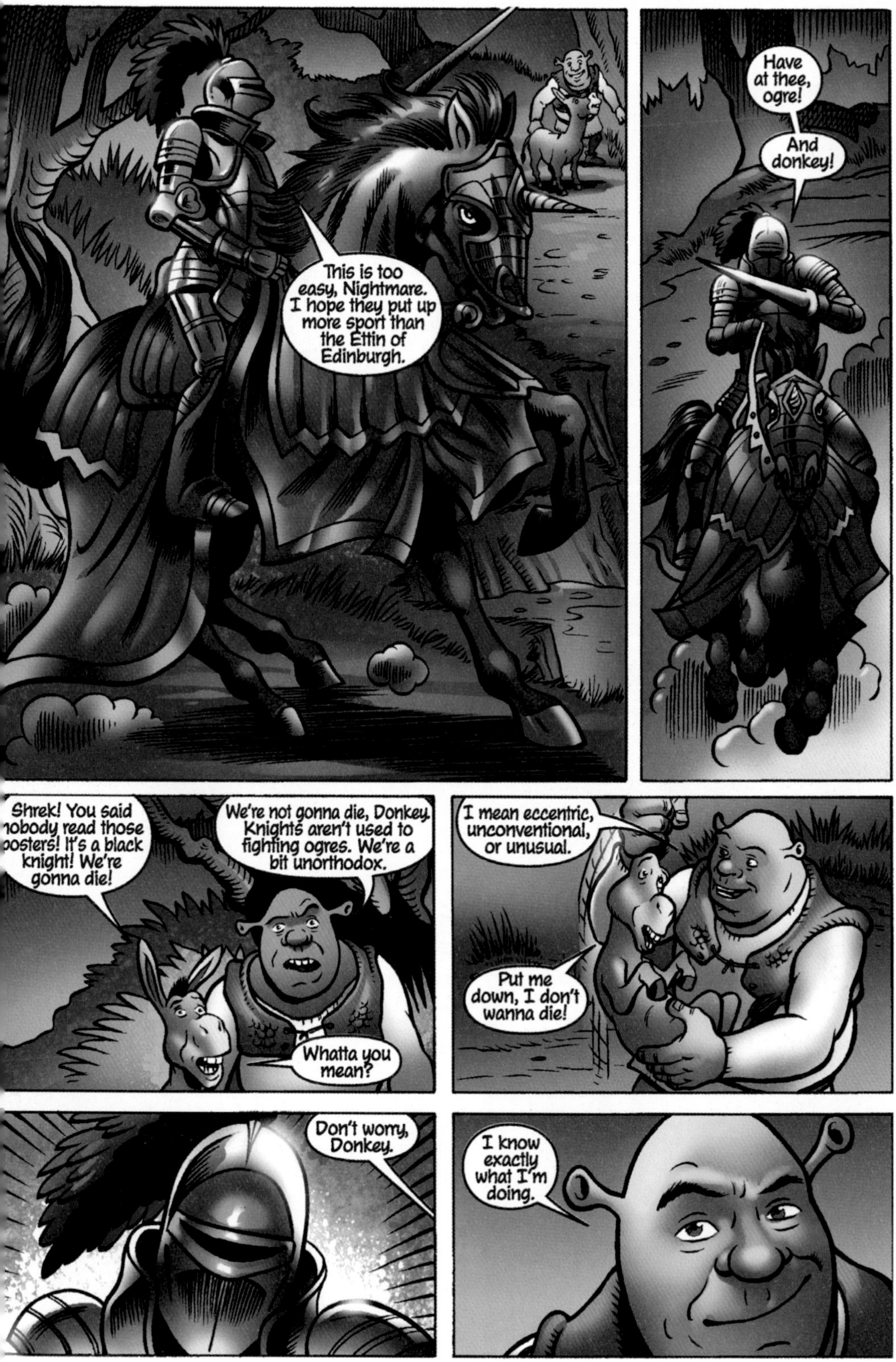
This is too easy, Nightmare. I hope they put up more sport than the Ettin of Edinburgh.
Have at thee, ogre!
And donkey!
Shrek! You said nobody read those posters! It's a black knight! We're gonna die!
We're not gonna die, Donkey. Knights aren't used to fighting ogres. We're a bit unorthodox.
Whatta you mean?
I mean eccentric, unconventional, or unusual.
Put me down, I don't wanna die!
Don't worry, Donkey.
I know exactly what I'm doing.

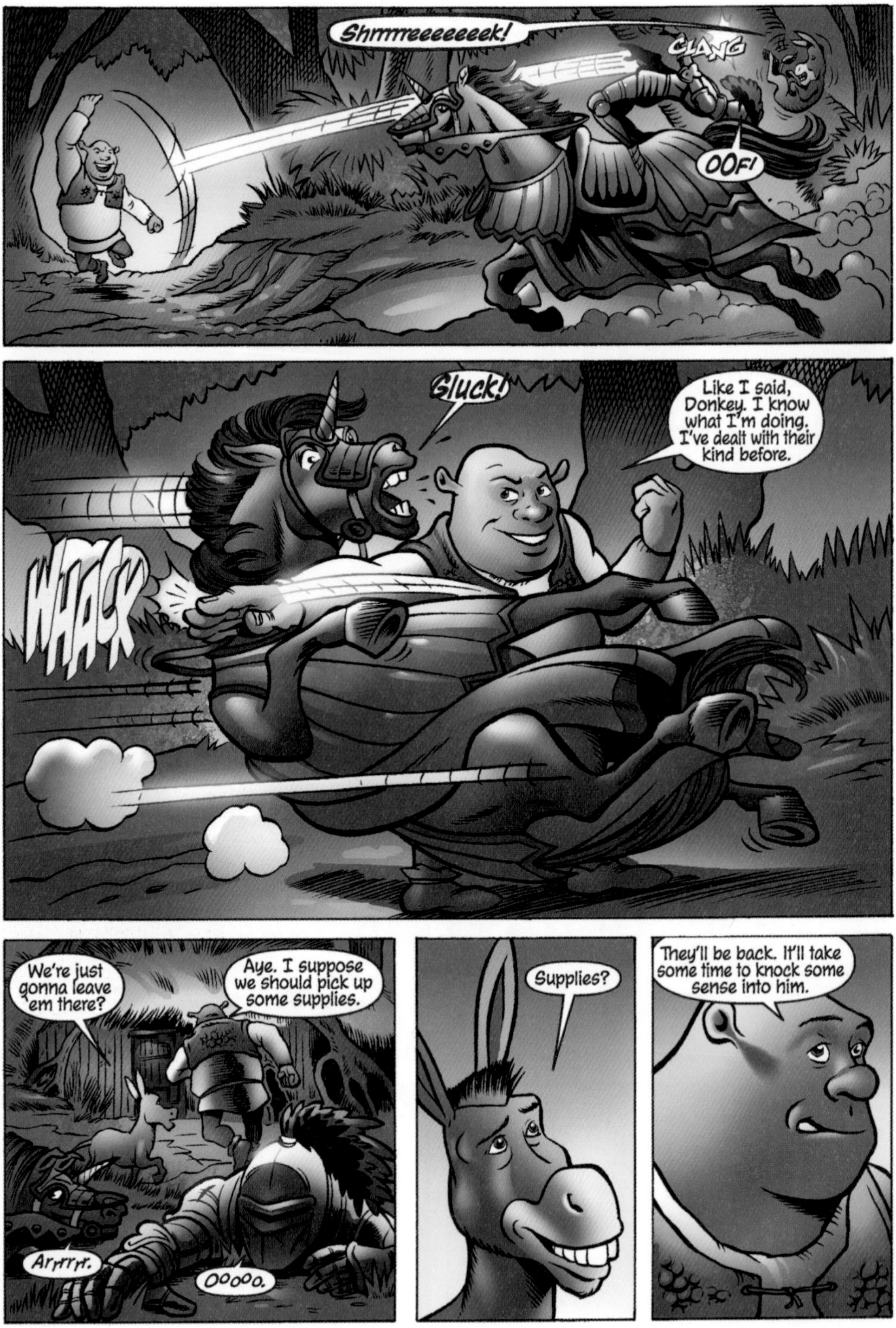
Shrrrreeeeeeeek!
CLANG
OOF!
GLUCK!
Like I said, Donkey. I know what I'm doing. I've dealt with their kind before.
WHACK
We're just gonna leave 'em there?
Aye. I suppose we should pick up some supplies.
Arrrrr.
Ooooo.
Supplies?
They'll be back. It'll take some time to knock some sense into him.

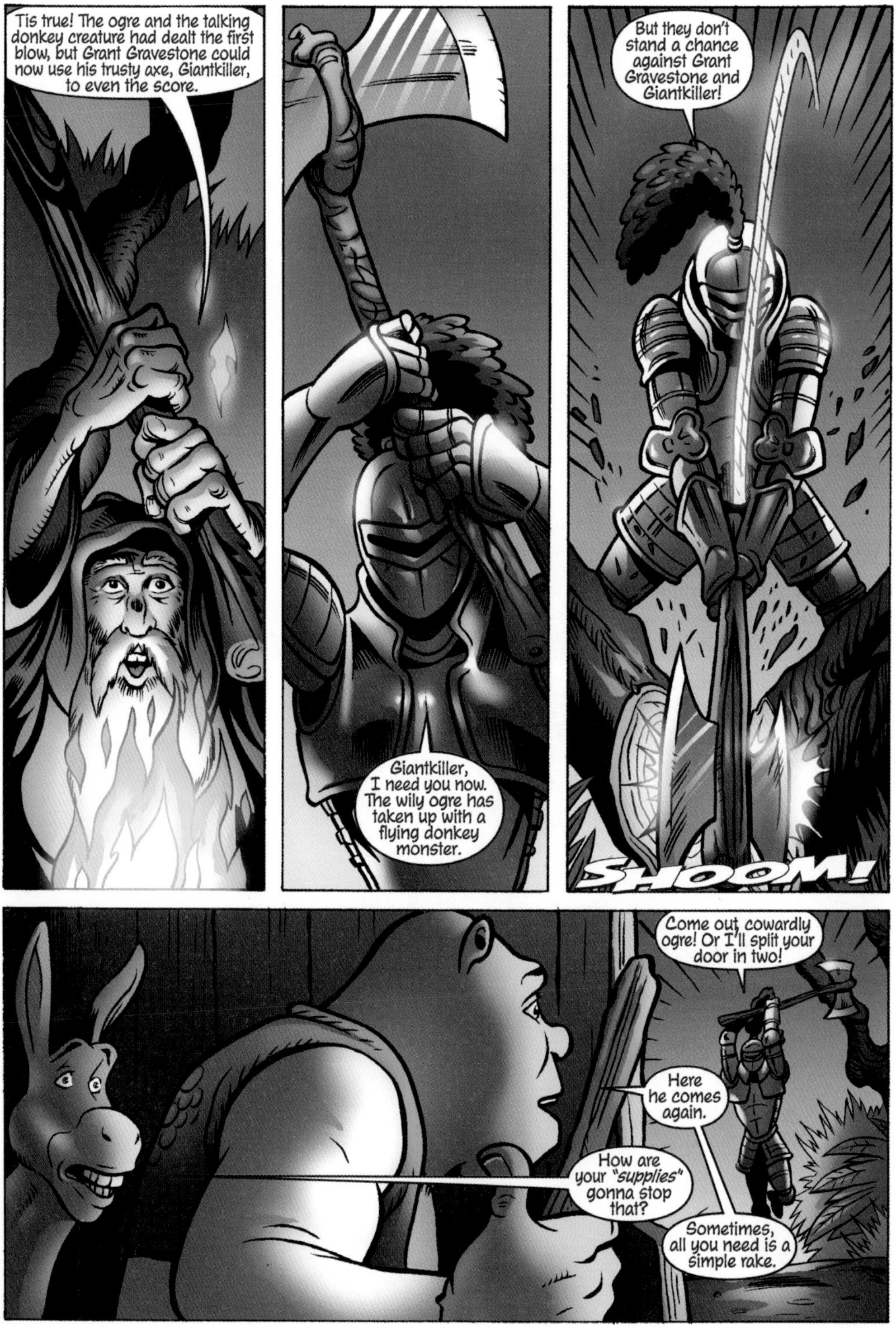
Tis true! The ogre and the talking donkey creature had dealt the first blow, but Grant Gravestone could now use his trusty axe, Giantkiller, to even the score.
Giantkiller, I need you now. The wily ogre has taken up with a flying donkey monster.
But they don't stand a chance against Grant Gravestone and Giantkiller!
SHOOM!
Come out, cowardly ogre! Or I'll split your door in two!
Here he comes again.
How are your "supplies" gonna stop that?
Sometimes, all you need is a simple rake.

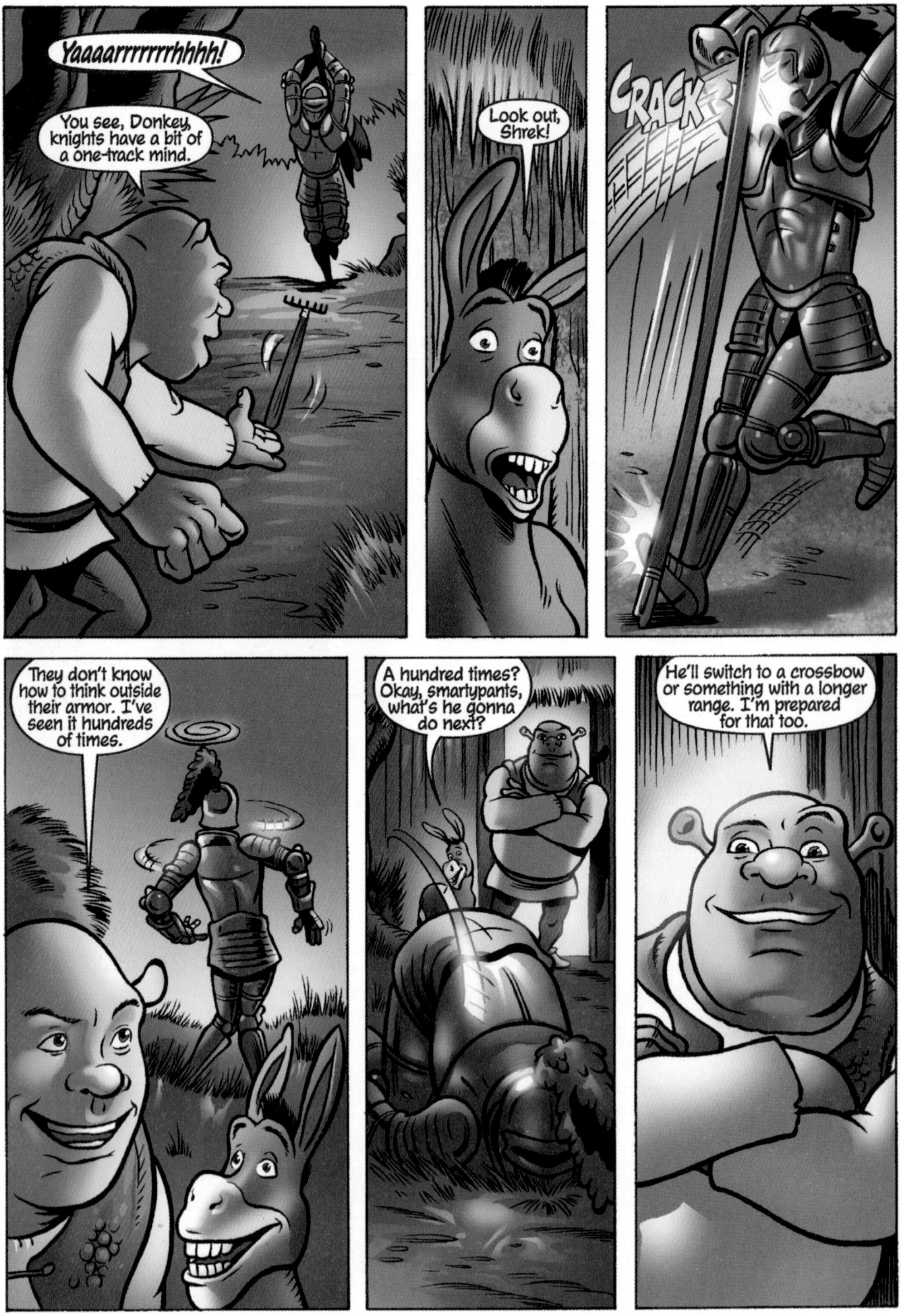
Yaaaarrrrrrrhhhh!
You see, Donkey, knights have a bit of a one-track mind.
Look out, Shrek!
CRACK
They don't know how to think outside their armor. I've seen it hundreds of times.
A hundred times? Okay, smartypants, what's he gonna do next?
He'll switch to a crossbow or something with a longer range. I'm prepared for that too.

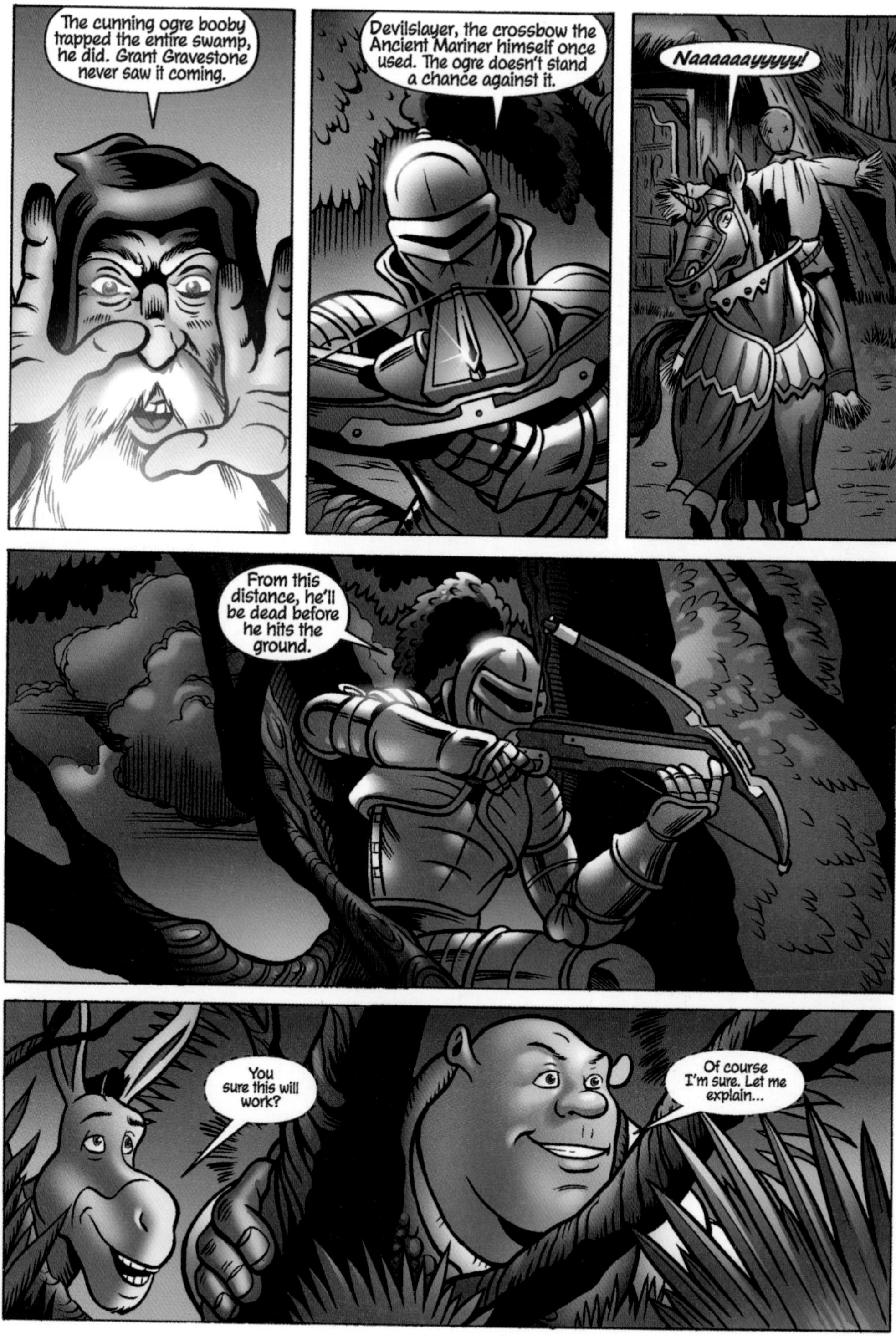
The cunning ogre booby trapped the entire swamp, he did. Grant Gravestone never saw it coming.
Devilslayer, the crossbow the Ancient Mariner himself once used. The ogre doesn't stand a chance against it.
Naaaaaayyyyy!
From this distance, he'll be dead before he hits the ground.
You sure this will work?
Of course I'm sure. Let me explain...

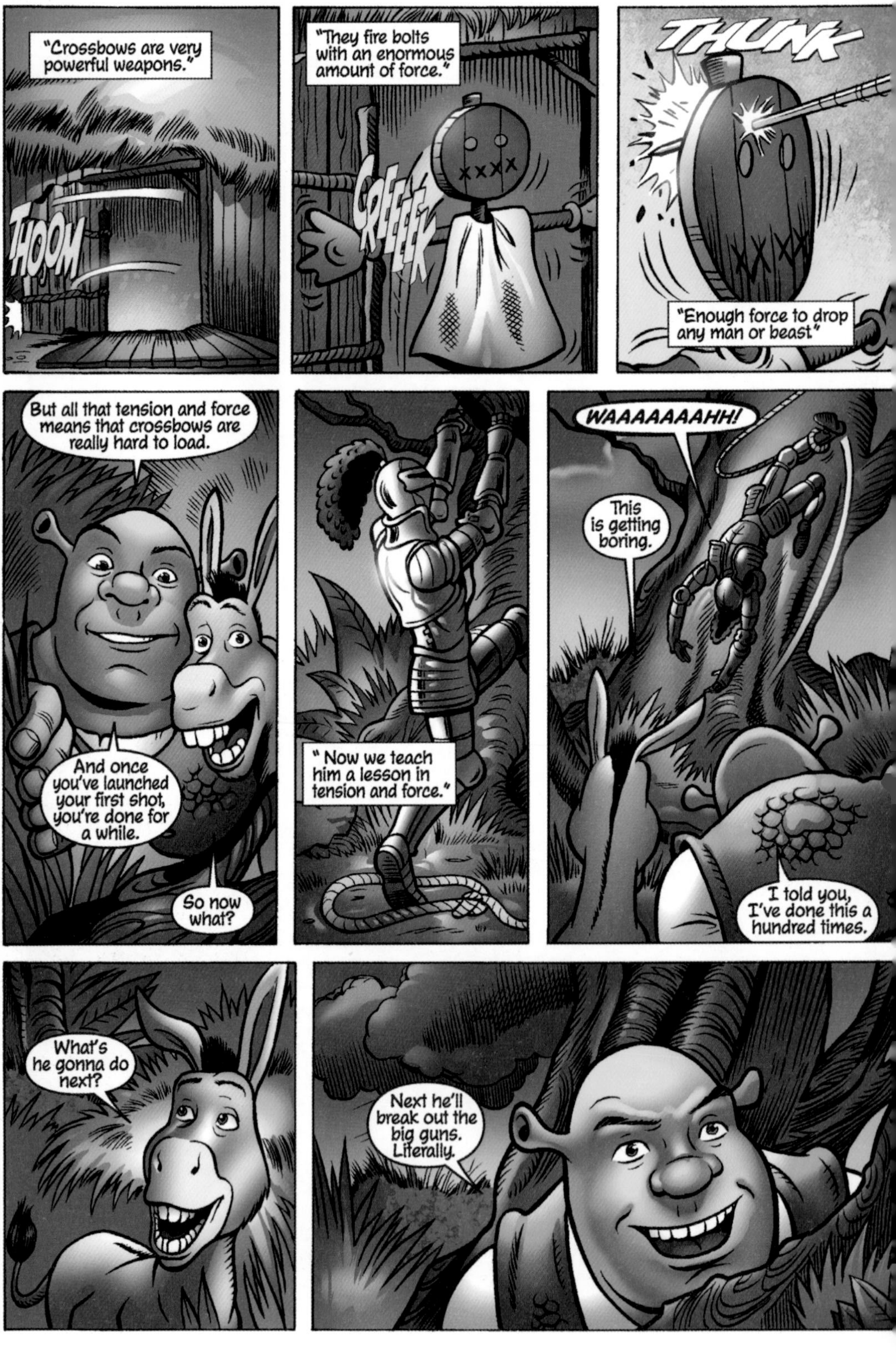
"Crossbows are very powerful weapons."
THOOM
"They fire bolts with an enormous amount of force."
CREEEEEK
THUNK
"Enough force to drop any man or beast."
But all that tension and force means that crossbows are really hard to load.
And once you've launched your first shot, you're done for a while.
So now what?
" Now we teach him a lesson in tension and force."
WAAAAAAAHH!
This is getting boring.
I told you, I've done this a hundred times.
What's he gonna do next?
Next he'll break out the big guns. Literally.

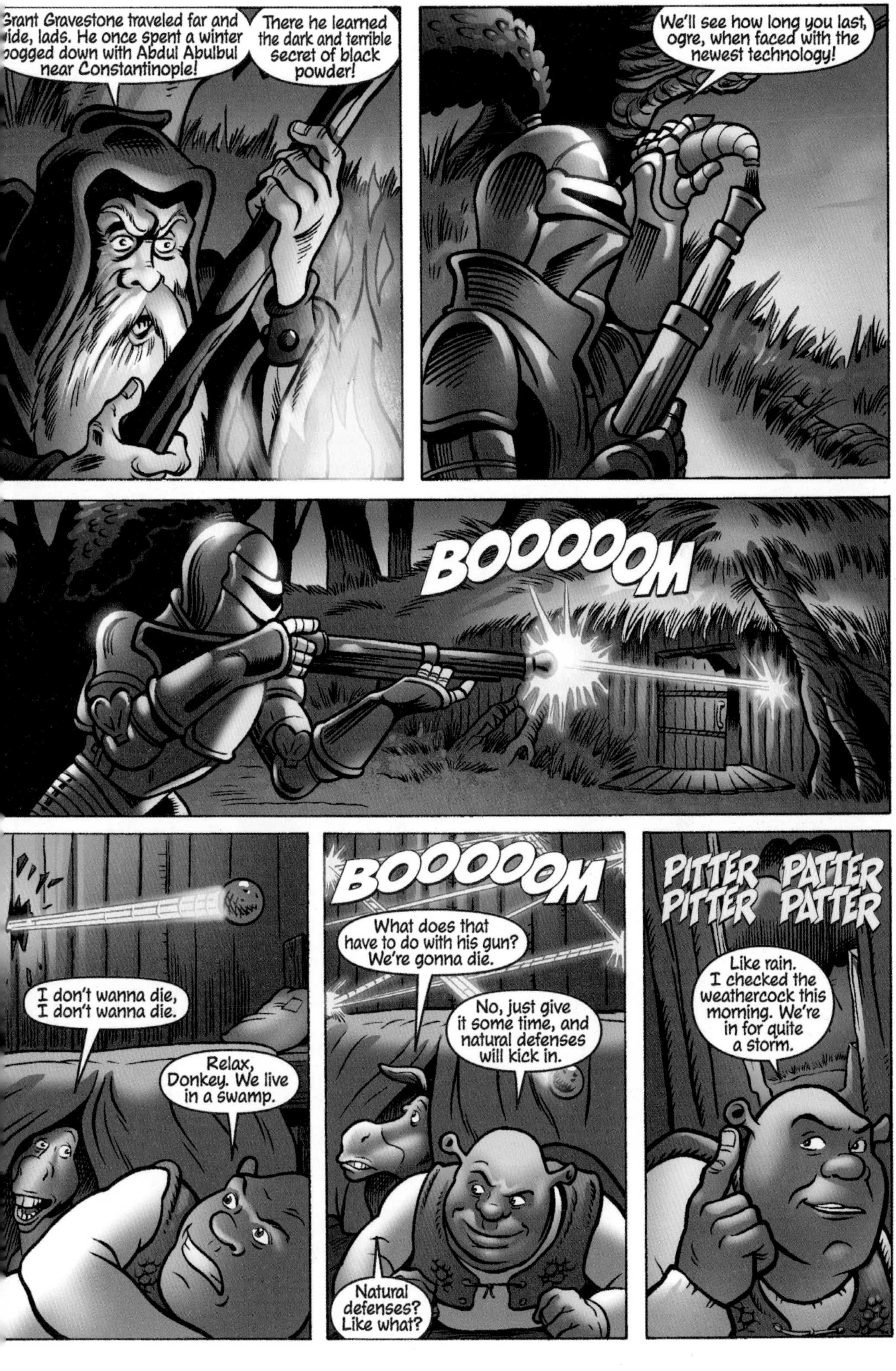
Grant Gravestone traveled far and wide, lads. He once spent a winter bogged down with Abdul Abulbul near Constantinople!
There he learned the dark and terrible secret of black powder!
We'll see how long you last, ogre, when faced with the newest technology!
BOOOOOOM
I don't wanna die, I don't wanna die.
Relax, Donkey. We live in a swamp.
BOOOOOOM
What does that have to do with his gun? We're gonna die.
No, just give it some time, and natural defenses will kick in.
Natural defenses? Like what?
PITTER PATTER PITTER PATTER
Like rain. I checked the weathercock this morning. We're in for quite a storm.

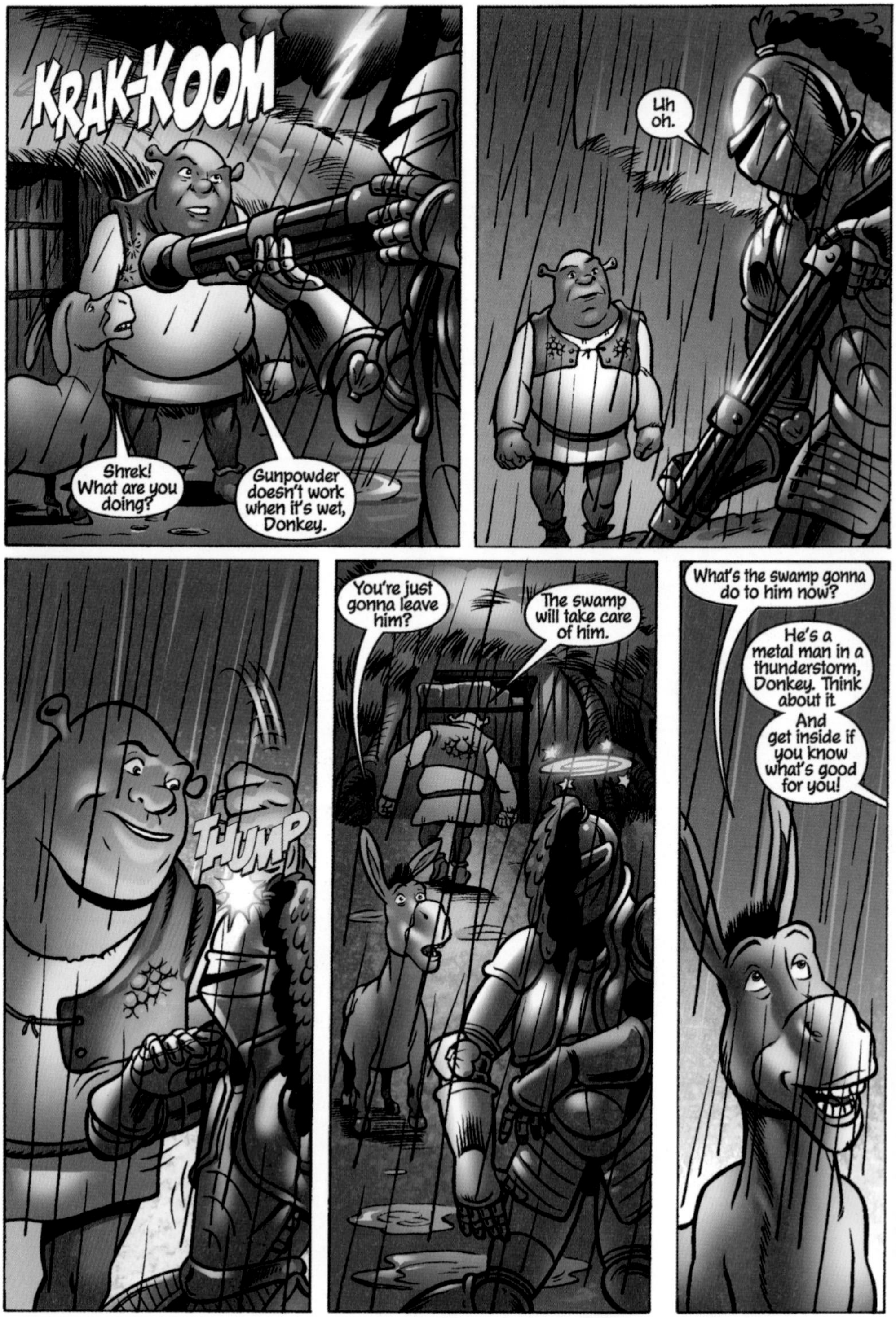
KRAK-KOOM
Shrek! What are you doing?
Gunpowder doesn't work when it's wet, Donkey.
Uh oh.
THUMP
You're just gonna leave him?
The swamp will take care of him.
What's the swamp gonna do to him now?
He's a metal man in a thunderstorm, Donkey. Think about it
And get inside if you know what's good for you!

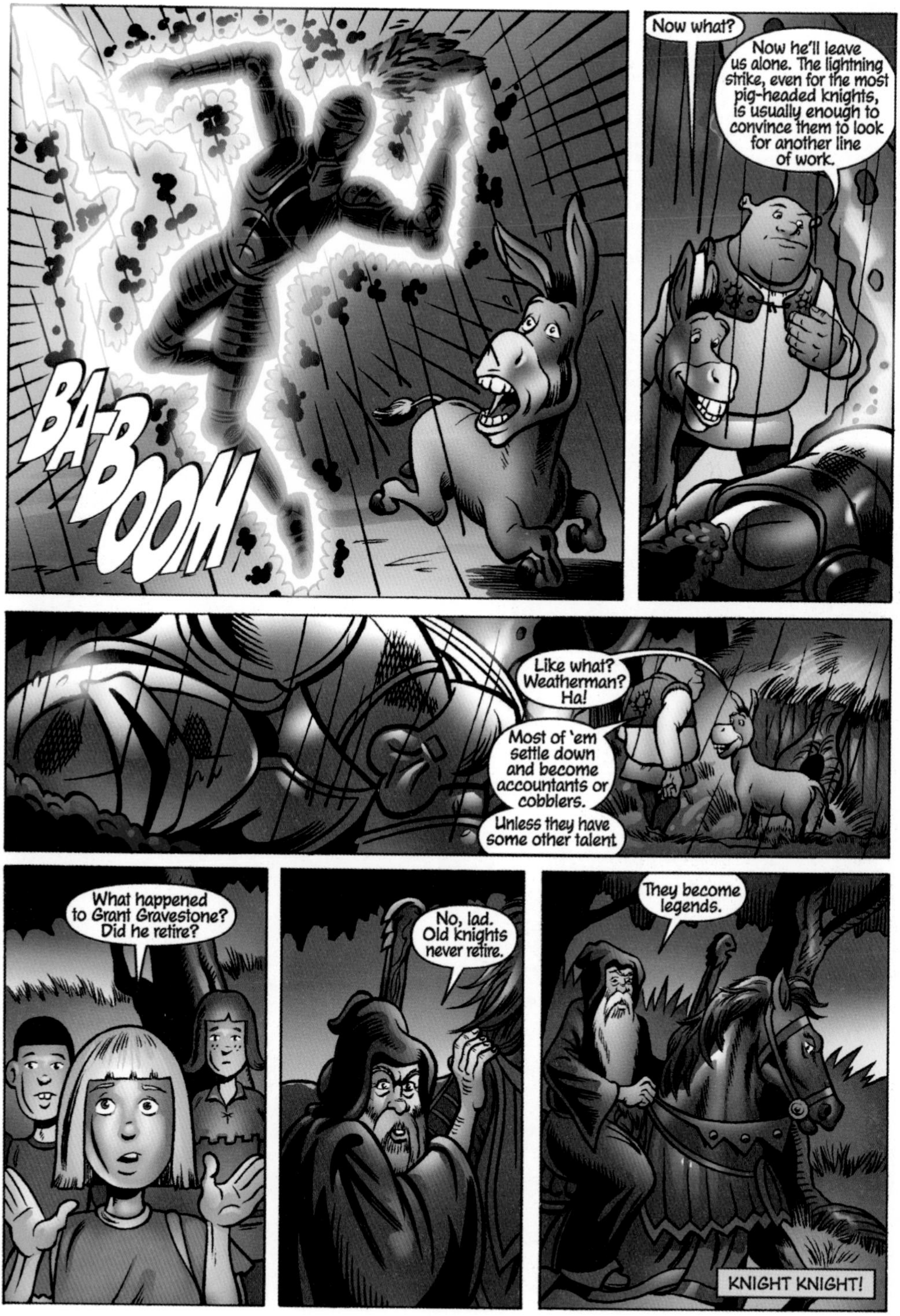
BA-BOOM
Now what?
Now he'll leave us alone. The lightning strike, even for the most pig-headed knights, is usually enough to convince them to look for another line of work.
Like what? Weatherman? Ha!
Most of 'em settle down and become accountants or cobblers.
Unless they have some other talent
What happened to Grant Gravestone? Did he retire?
No, lad. Old knights never retire.
They become legends.
KNIGHT KNIGHT!

LET THEM EAT CAKE

WRITERS **ANDREW DABB**
PENCILS **MAGIC EYE STUDIOS**
INKS **BAMBOS GEORGIOU**
COLORS **KEV HOPGOOD**
LETTERS **JIMMY BETANCOURT/COMICRAFT**

LET THEM EAT CAKE

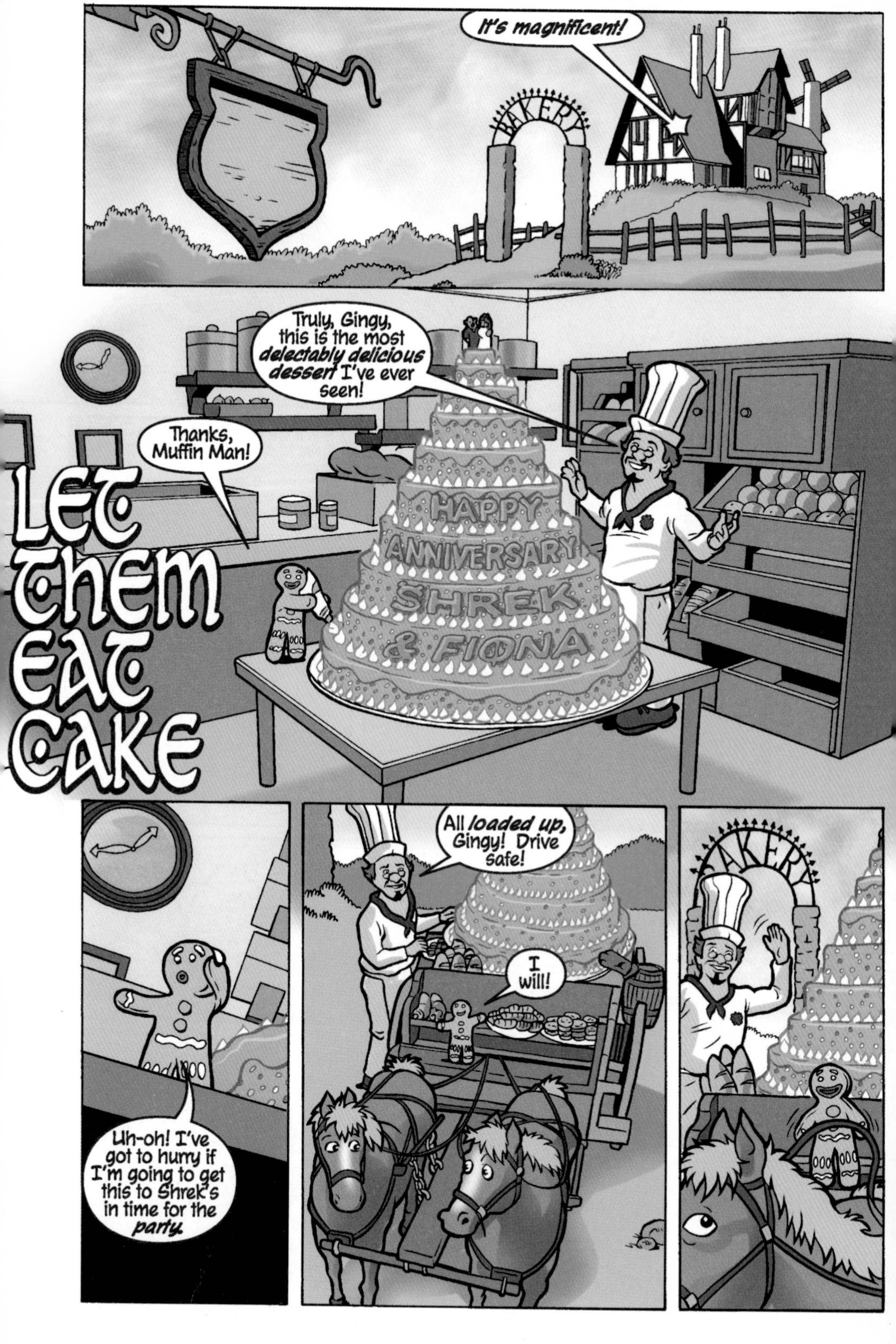
BAKERY
It's magnificent!
Truly, Gingy, this is the most *delectably delicious dessert* I've ever seen!
Thanks, Muffin Man!
HAPPY ANNIVERSARY SHREK & FIONA
Uh-oh! I've got to hurry if I'm going to get this to Shrek's in time for the *party.*
All *loaded up,* Gingy! Drive safe!
I will!

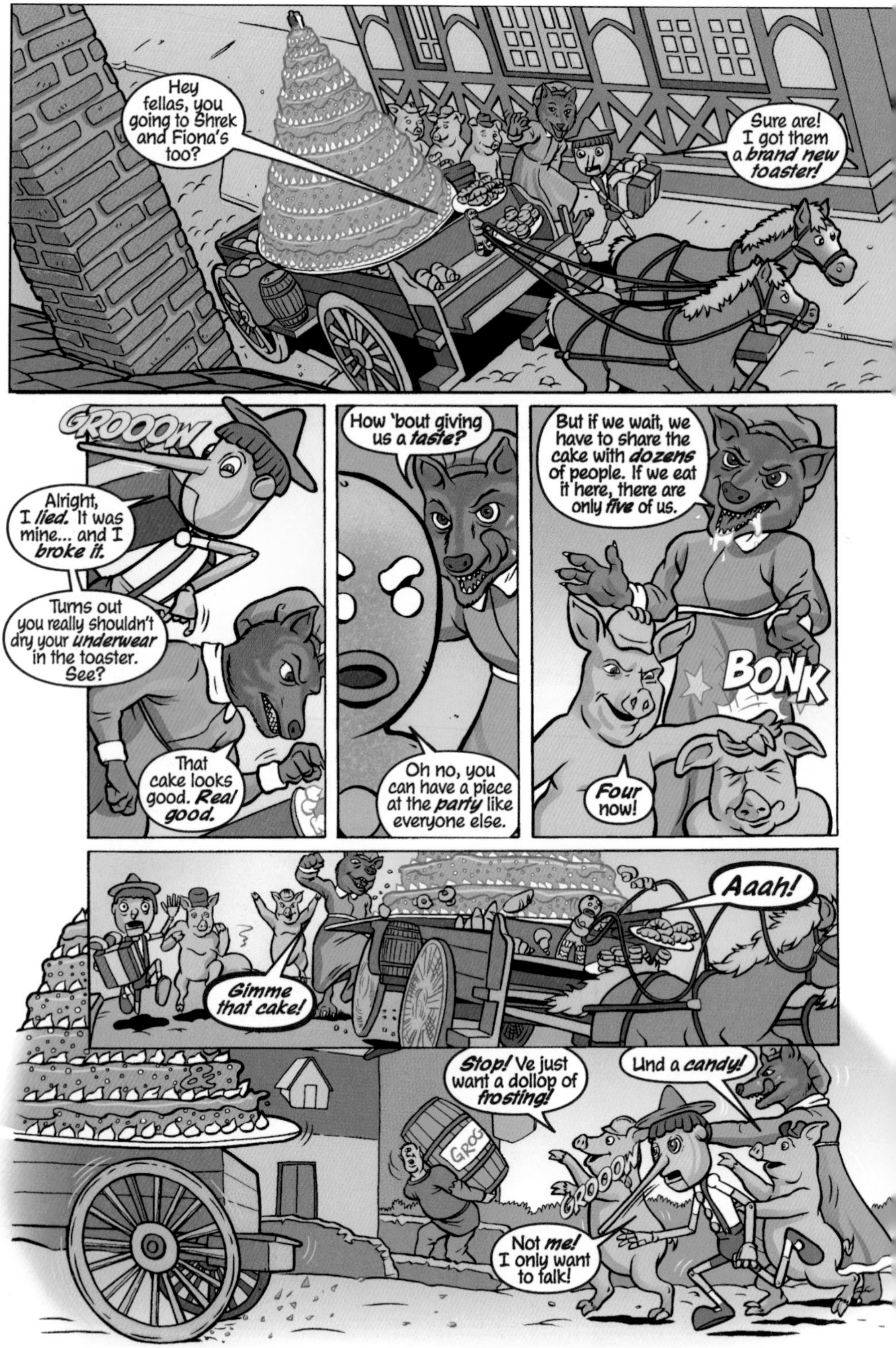
Hey fellas, you going to Shrek and Fiona's too?
Sure are! I got them a brand new toaster!
GROOOW
Alright, I lied. It was mine... and I broke it.
Turns out you really shouldn't dry your underwear in the toaster. See?
That cake looks good. Real good.
How 'bout giving us a taste?
Oh no, you can have a piece at the party like everyone else.
But if we wait, we have to share the cake with dozens of people. If we eat it here, there are only five of us.
BONK
Four now!
Aaah!
Gimme that cake!
GROG
Stop! Ve just want a dollop of frosting!
Und a candy!
GROOOW
Not me! I only want to talk!

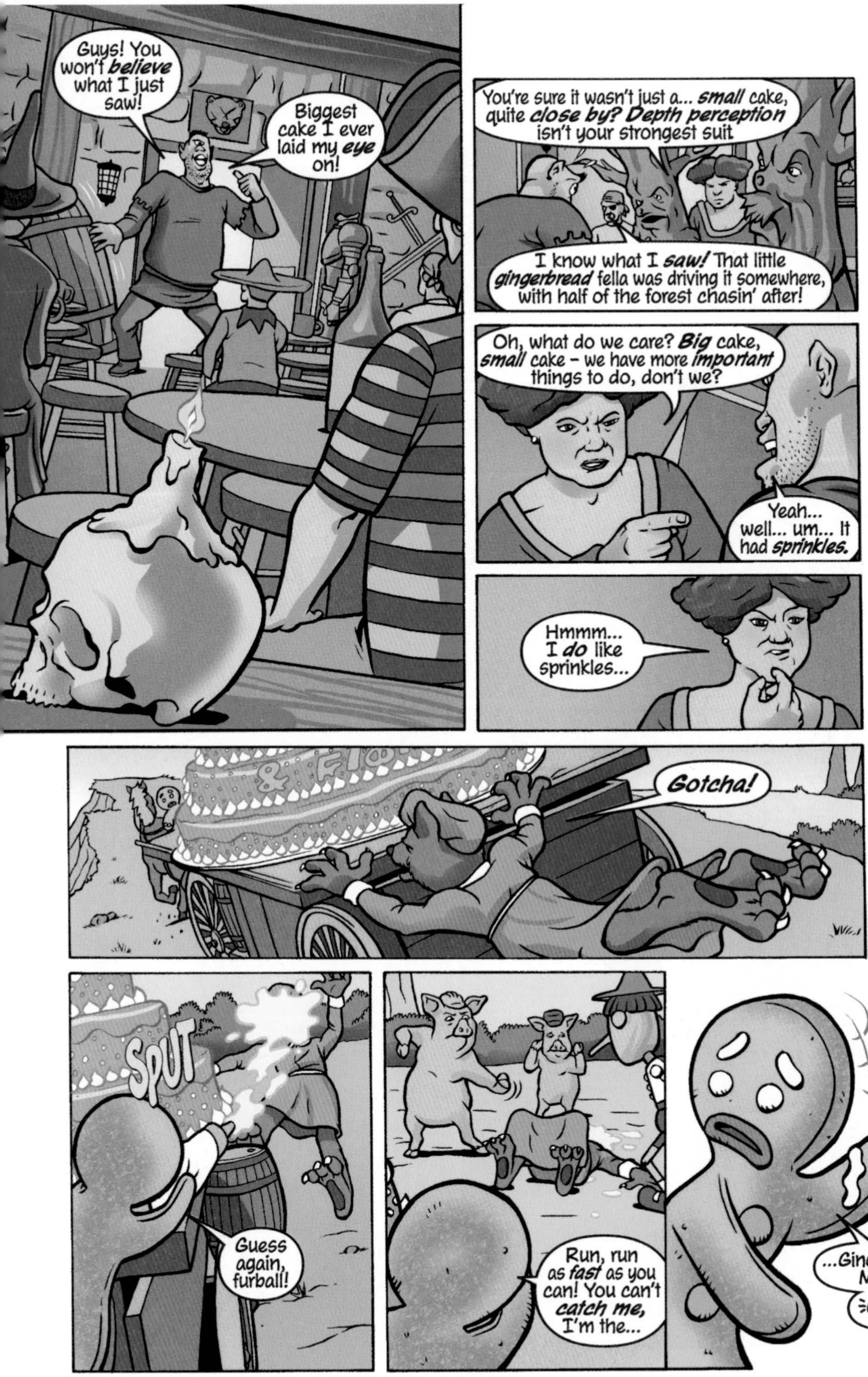
Guys! You won't *believe* what I just saw!
Biggest cake I ever laid my *eye* on!
You're sure it wasn't just a... *small* cake, quite *close by? Depth perception* isn't your strongest suit
I know what I *saw!* That little *gingerbread* fella was driving it somewhere, with half of the forest chasin' after!
Oh, what do we care? *Big* cake, *small* cake – we have more *important* things to do, don't we?
Yeah... well... um... It had *sprinkles.*
Hmmm... I *do* like sprinkles...
Gotcha!
SPUT
Guess again, furball!
Run, run as *fast* as you can! You can't *catch me,* I'm the...
...Gingerbread Man.
gulp

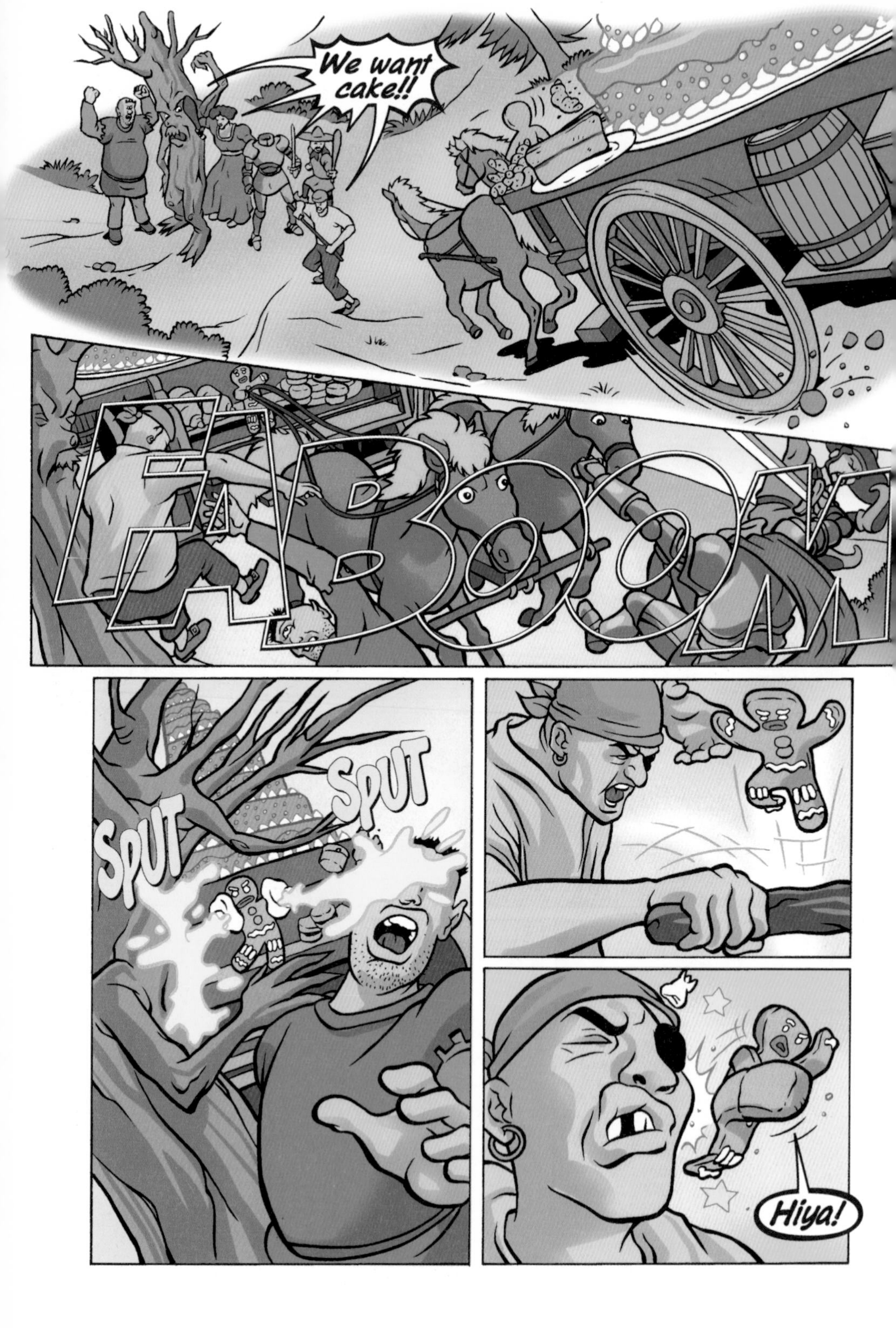
We want cake!!
KA-BOOOM
SPUT
SPUT
Hiya!

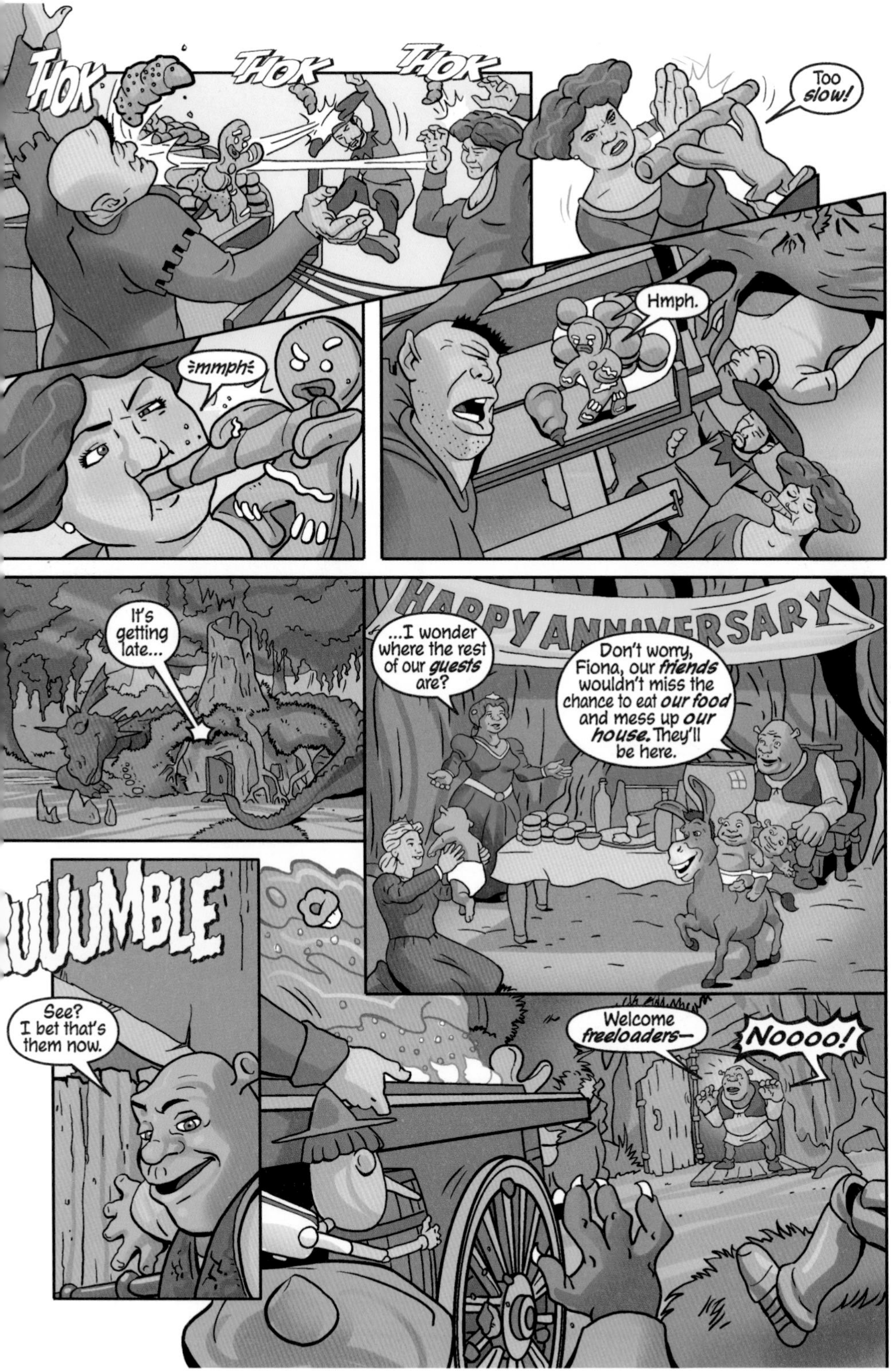
THOK
THOK
THOK
Too slow!
mmph
Hmph.
It's getting late...
HAPPY ANNIVERSARY
...I wonder where the rest of our guests are?
Don't worry, Fiona, our friends wouldn't miss the chance to eat our food and mess up our house. They'll be here.
UUUMBLE
See? I bet that's them now.
Welcome freeloaders—
Noooo!

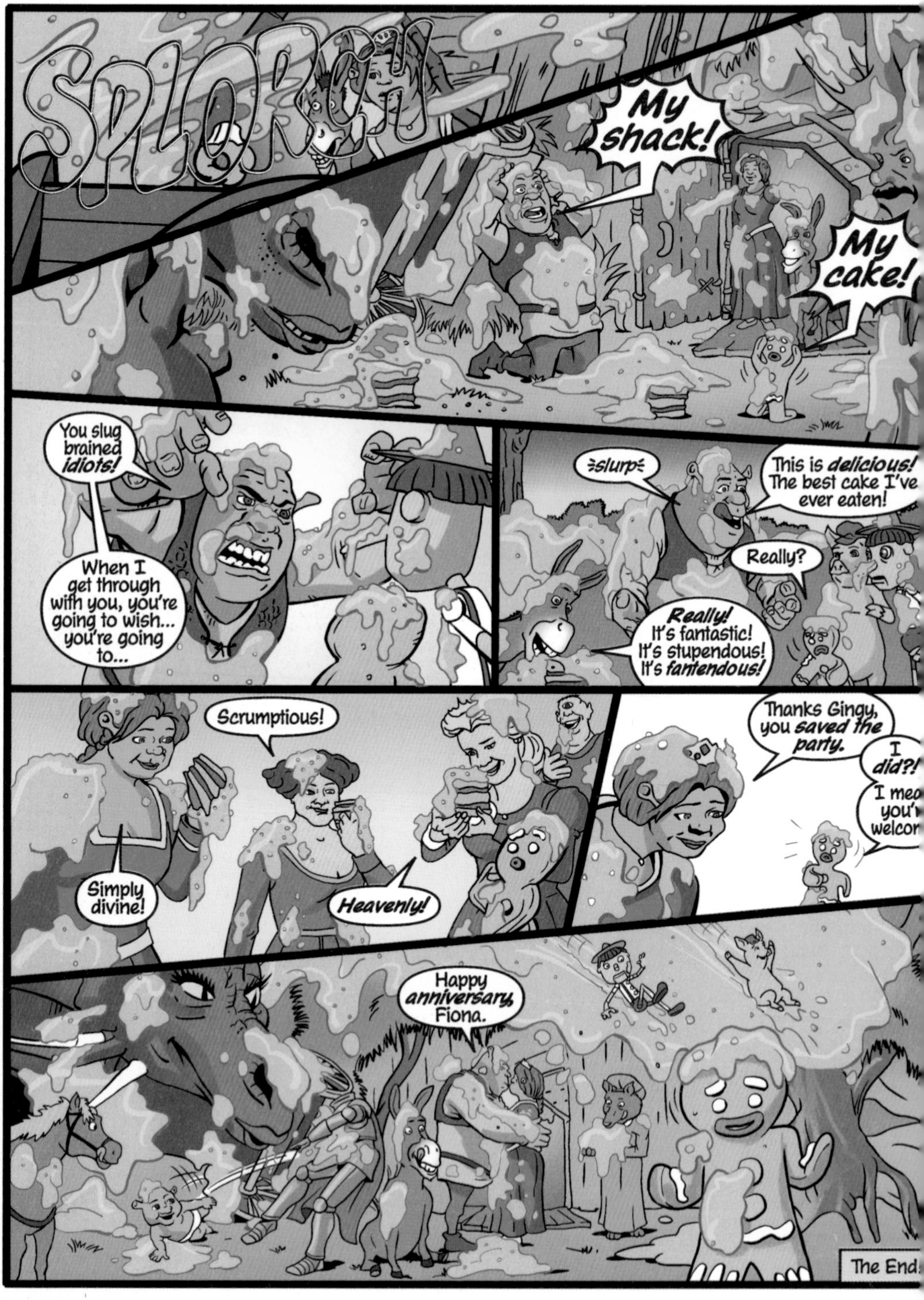
SPLORCH
My shack!
My cake!
You slug brained *idiots!*
When I get through with you, you're going to wish... you're going to...
≈slurp≈
This is *delicious!* The best cake I've ever eaten!
Really?
Really! It's fantastic! It's stupendous! It's *fantendous!*
Scrumptious!
Simply divine!
Heavenly!
Thanks Gingy, you *saved the party.*
I *did?!*
Happy *anniversary,* Fiona.
The End!

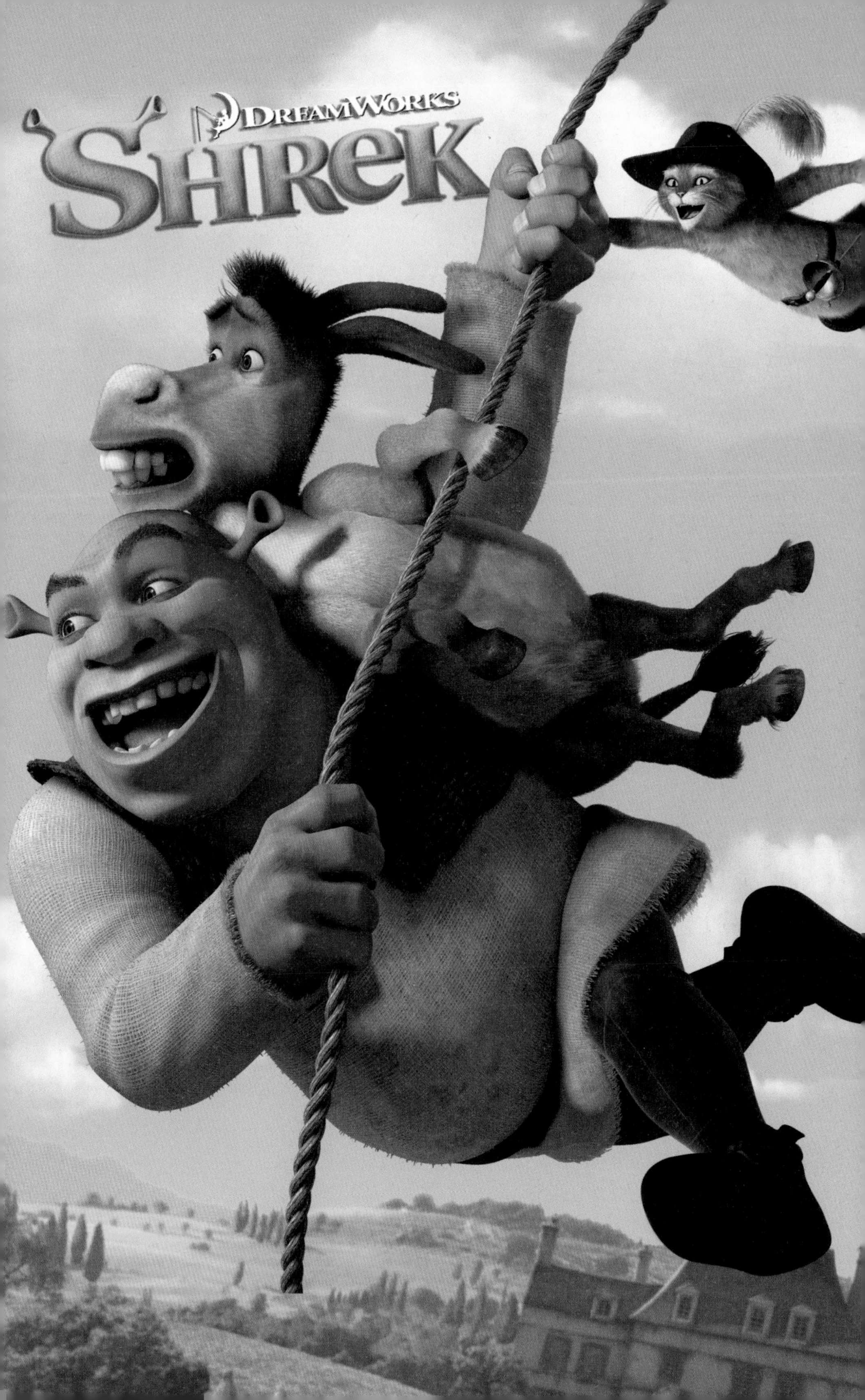
DreamWorks
Shrek

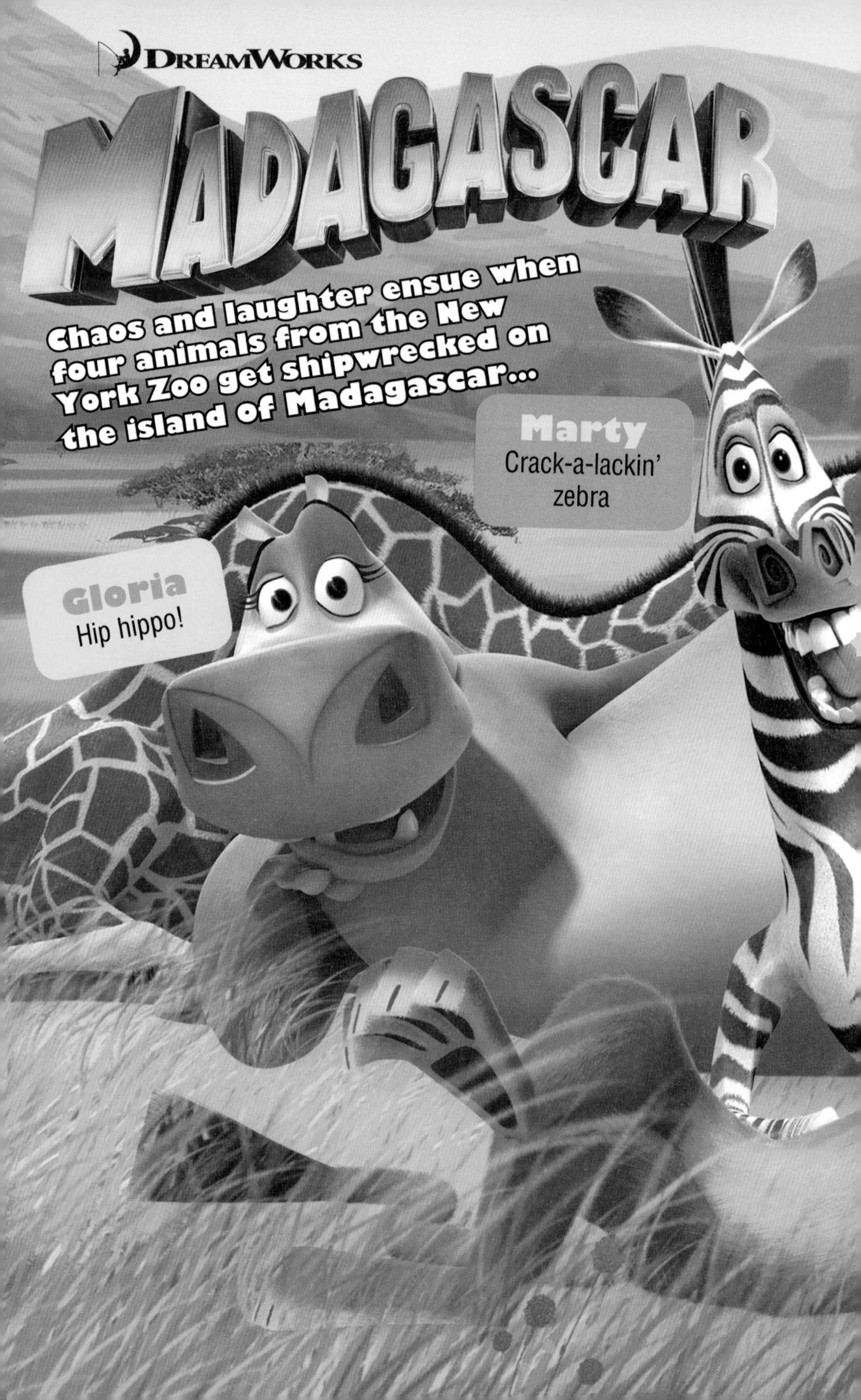
DreamWorks
MADAGASCAR
Chaos and laughter ensue when four animals from the New York Zoo get shipwrecked on the island of Madagascar...
Marty
Crack-a-lackin' zebra
Gloria
Hip hippo!

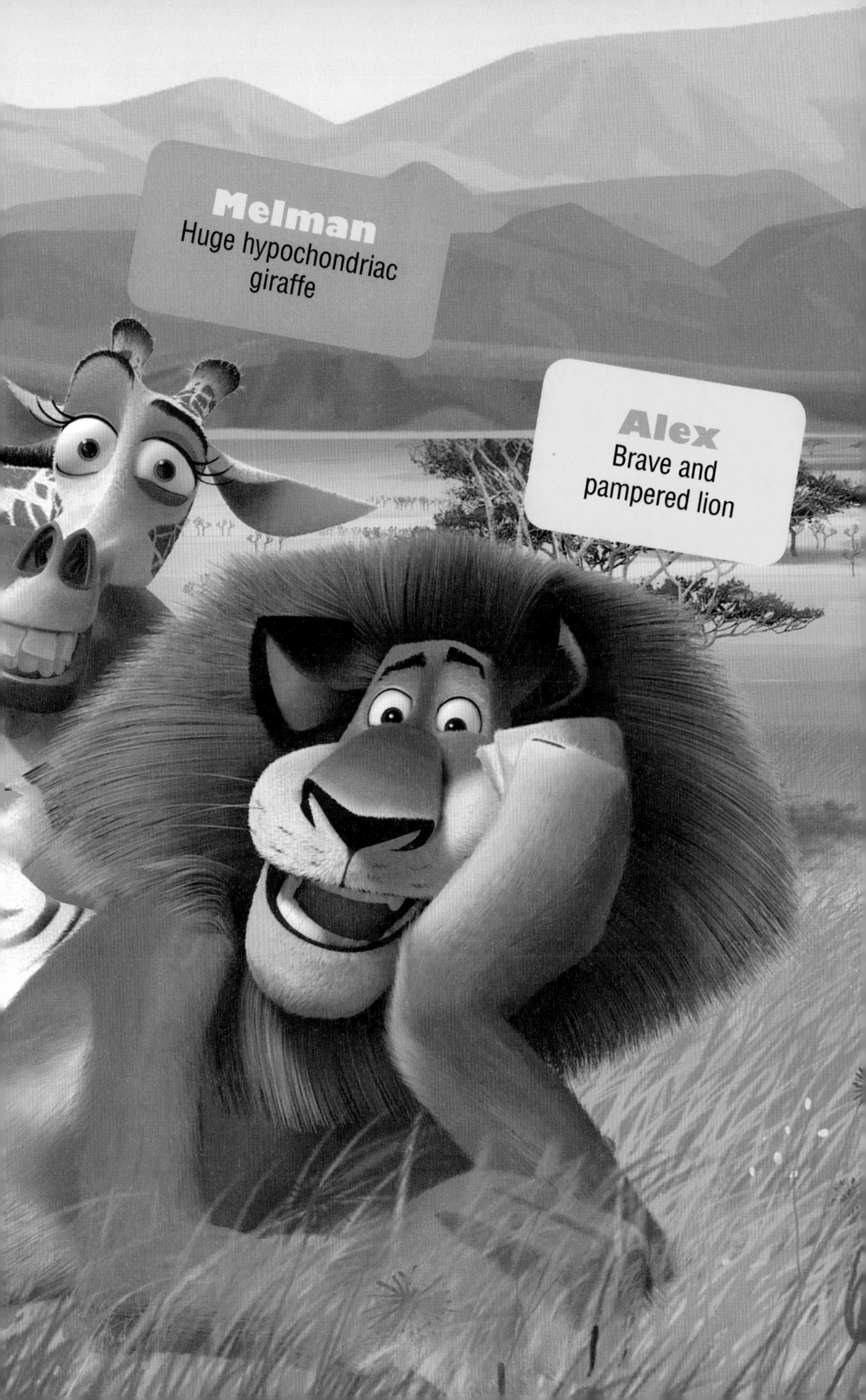
Melman
Huge hypochondriac giraffe
Alex
Brave and pampered lion

THE PERFECT GIFT

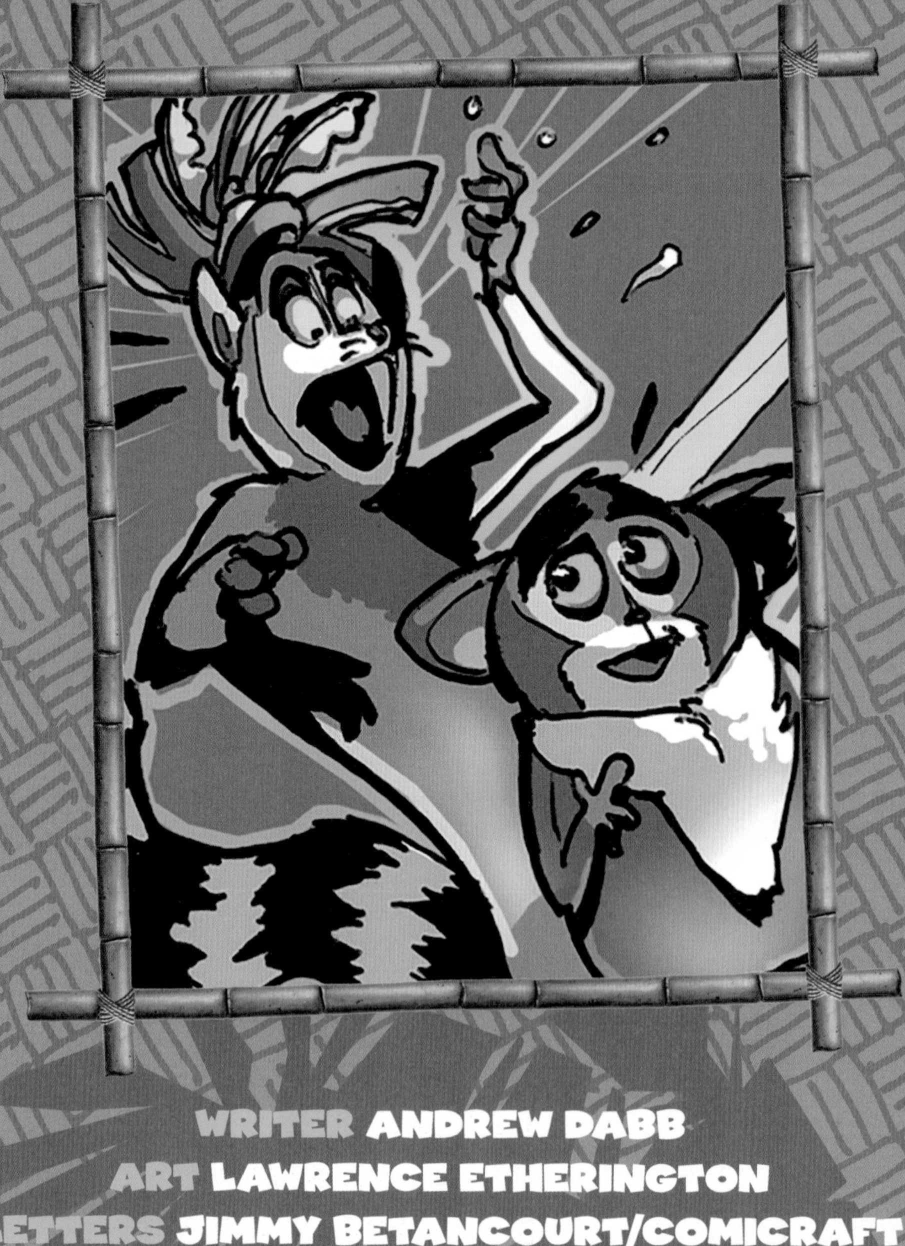

WRITER ANDREW DABB
ART LAWRENCE ETHERINGTON
LETTERS JIMMY BETANCOURT/COMICRAFT

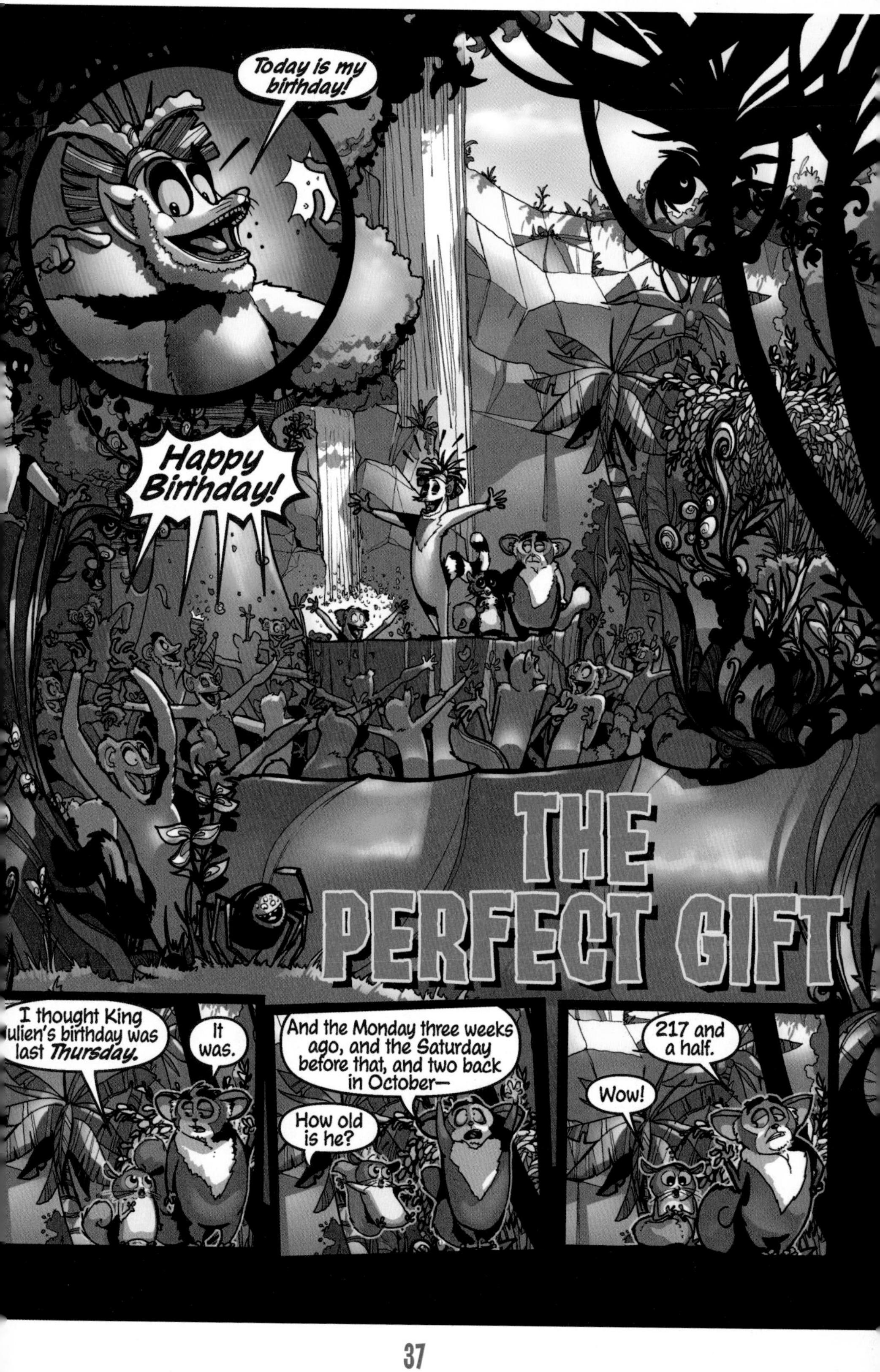
Today is my birthday!
Happy Birthday!
THE PERFECT GIFT
I thought King Julien's birthday was last *Thursday.*
It was.
And the Monday three weeks ago, and the Saturday before that, and two back in October—
How old is he?
217 and a half.
Wow!

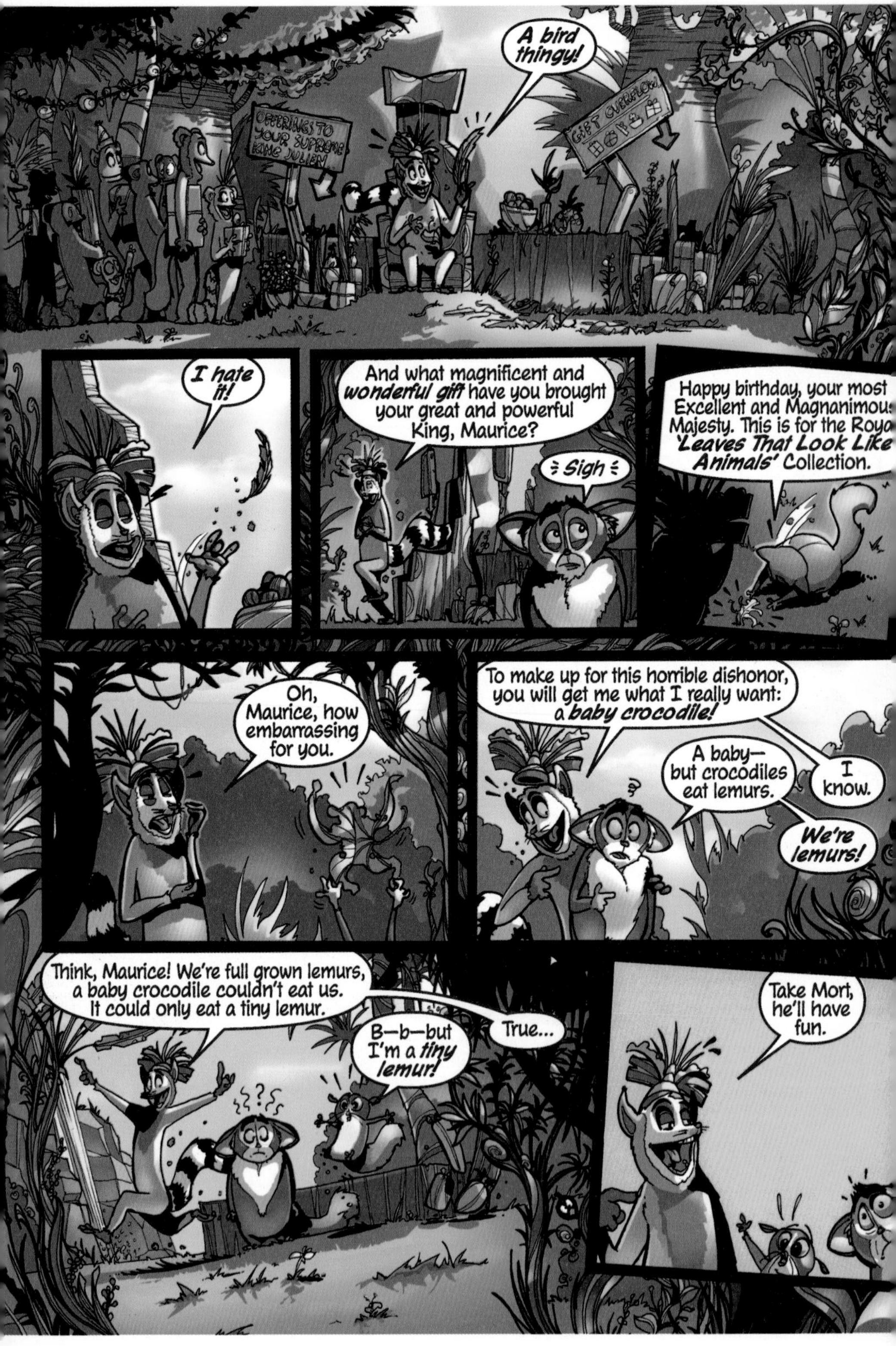
OFFERINGS TO YOUR SUPREME KING JULIEN
GIFT OVERFLOW
A bird thingy!
I hate it!
And what magnificent and wonderful gift have you brought your great and powerful King, Maurice?
Sigh
Happy birthday, your most Excellent and Magnanimous Majesty. This is for the Royal 'Leaves That Look Like Animals' Collection.
Oh, Maurice, how embarrassing for you.
To make up for this horrible dishonor, you will get me what I really want: a baby crocodile!
A baby— but crocodiles eat lemurs.
I know.
We're lemurs!
Think, Maurice! We're full grown lemurs, a baby crocodile couldn't eat us. It could only eat a tiny lemur.
True...
B—b—but I'm a tiny lemur!
Take Mort, he'll have fun.

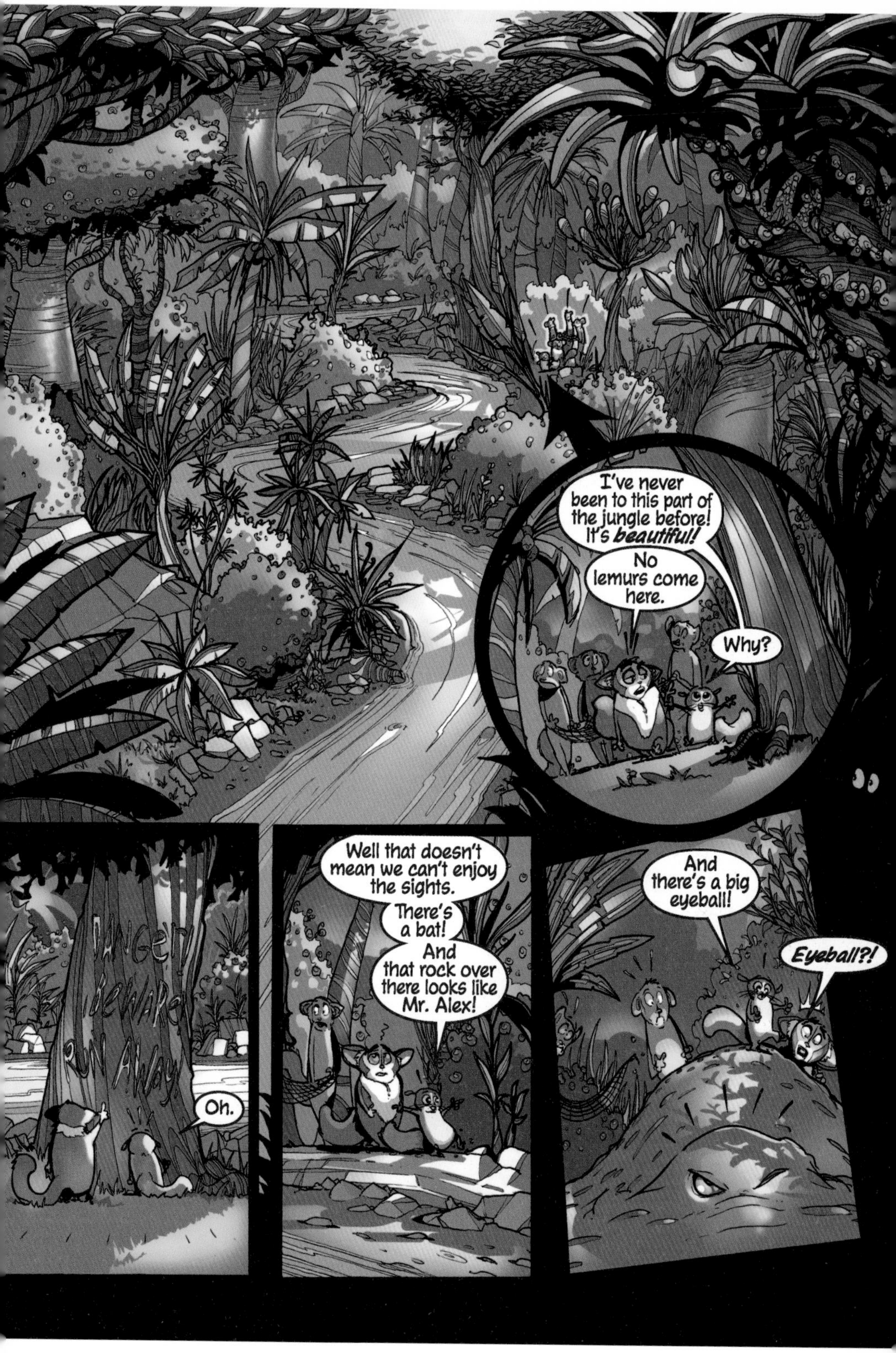
I've never been to this part of the jungle before! It's *beautiful!*
No lemurs come here.
Why?
DANGER!
BEWARE!
RUN AWAY
Oh.
Well that doesn't mean we can't enjoy the sights.
There's a bat!
And that rock over there looks like Mr. Alex!
And there's a big eyeball!
Eyeball?!

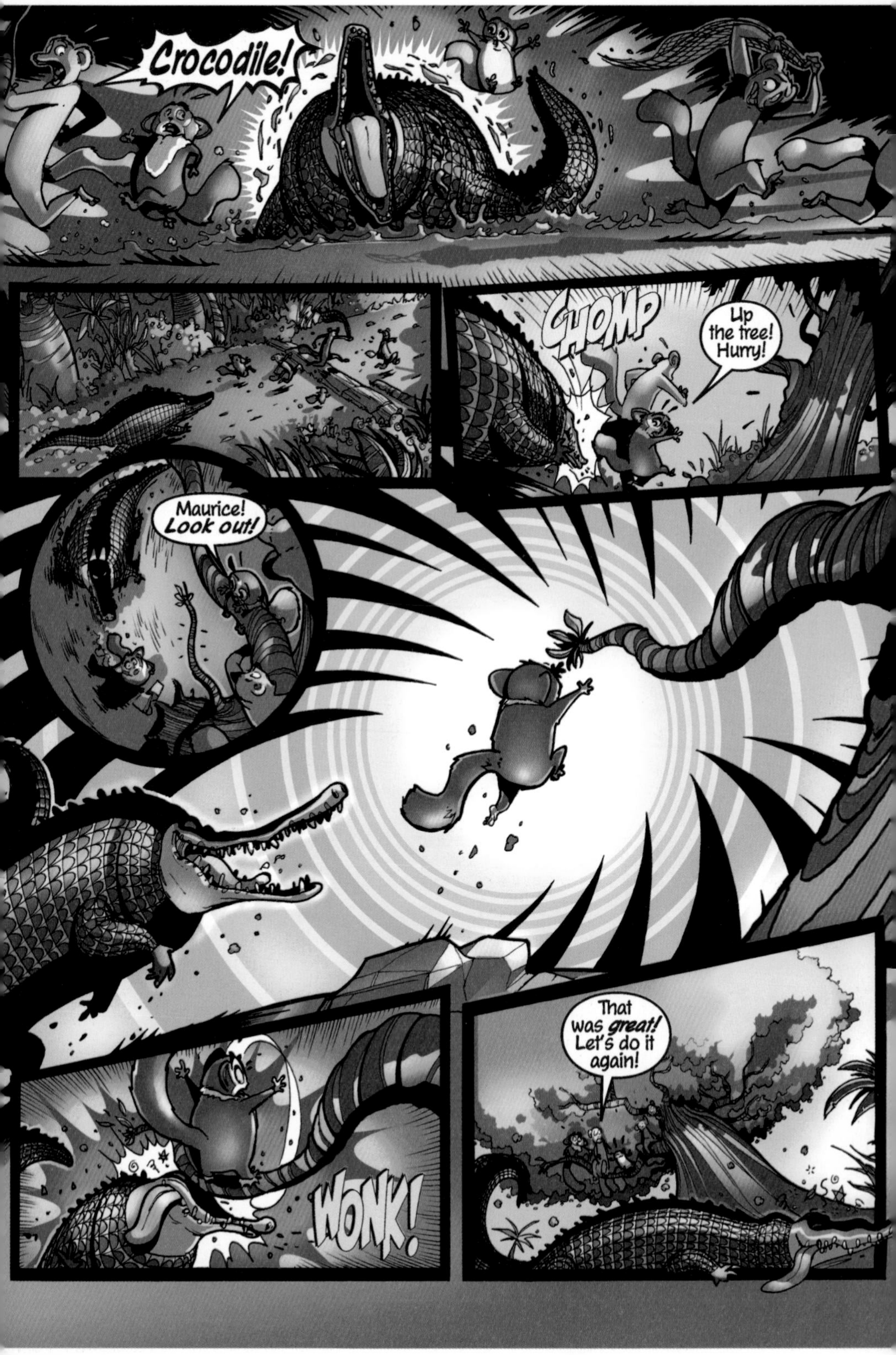
Crocodile!
CHOMP
Up the tree! Hurry!
Maurice! Look out!
WONK!
That was great! Let's do it again!

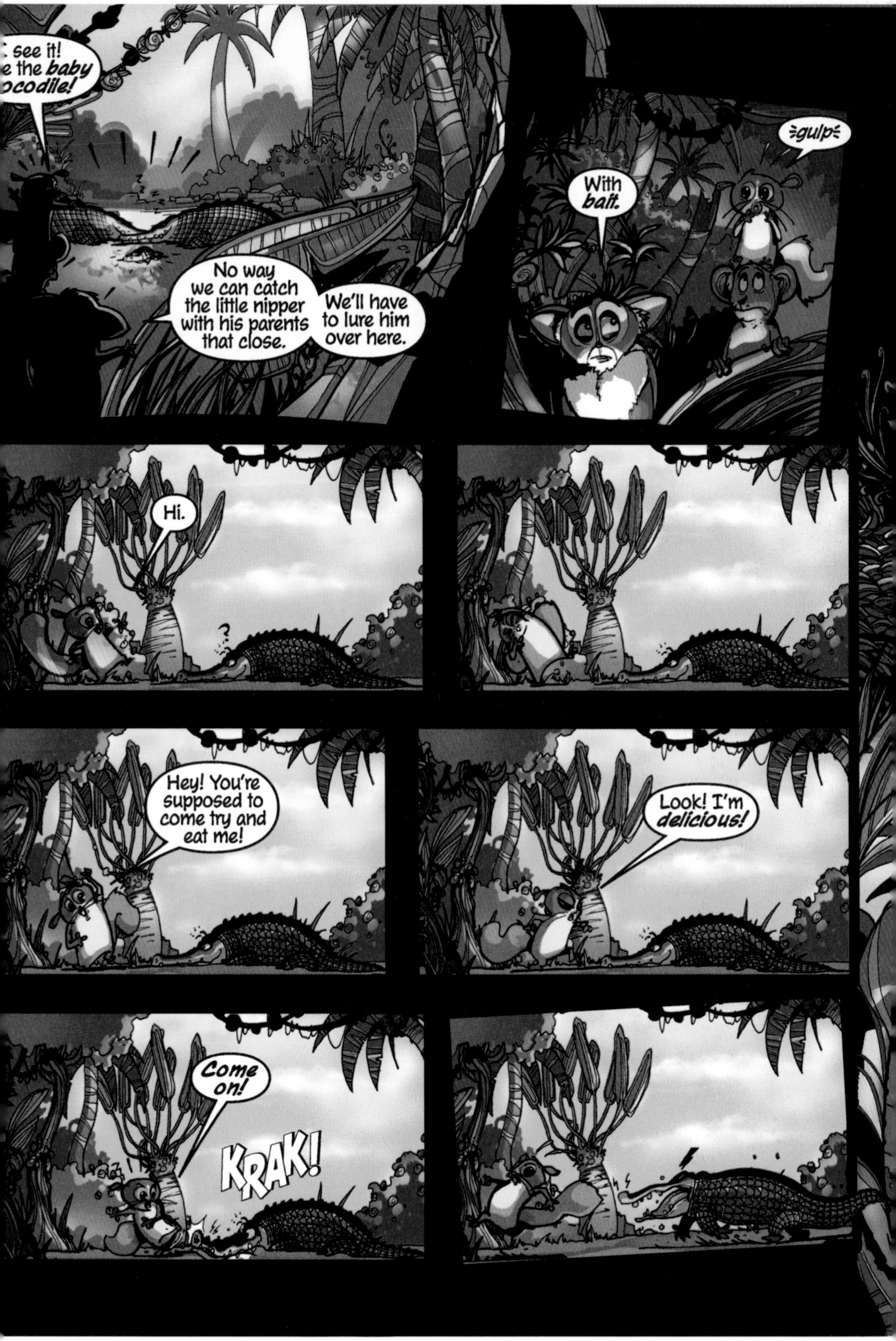
see it! e the baby ocodile!
No way we can catch the little nipper with his parents that close.
We'll have to lure him over here.
With bait.
gulp
Hi.
Hey! You're supposed to come try and eat me!
Look! I'm delicious!
Come on!
KRAK!

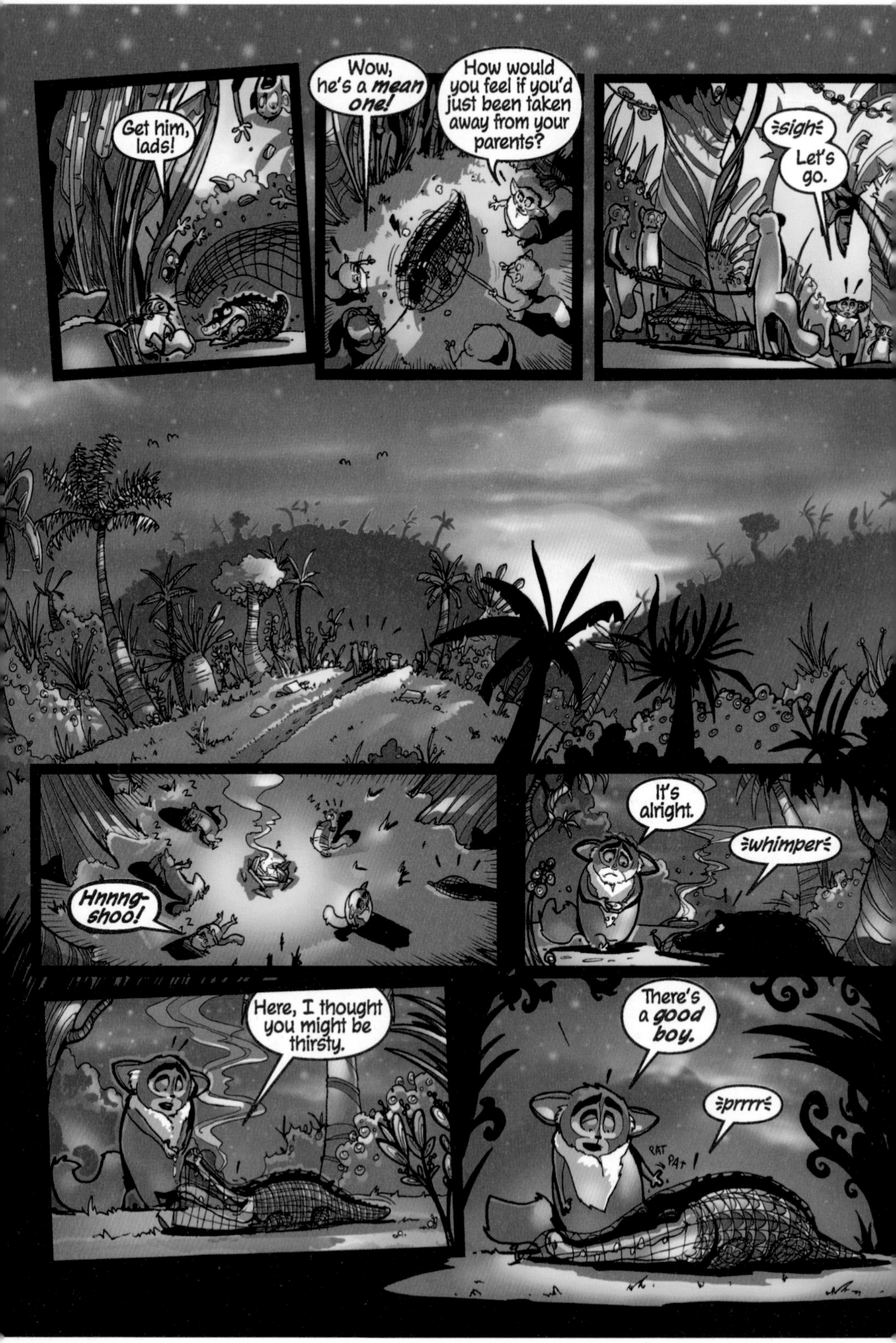

Get him, lads!
Wow, he's a ***mean one!***
How would you feel if you'd just been taken away from your parents?
≈sigh≈
Let's go.
Hnnng-shoo!
It's alright.
≈whimper≈
Here, I thought you might be thirsty.
There's a ***good boy.***
≈prrrr≈
PAT PAT

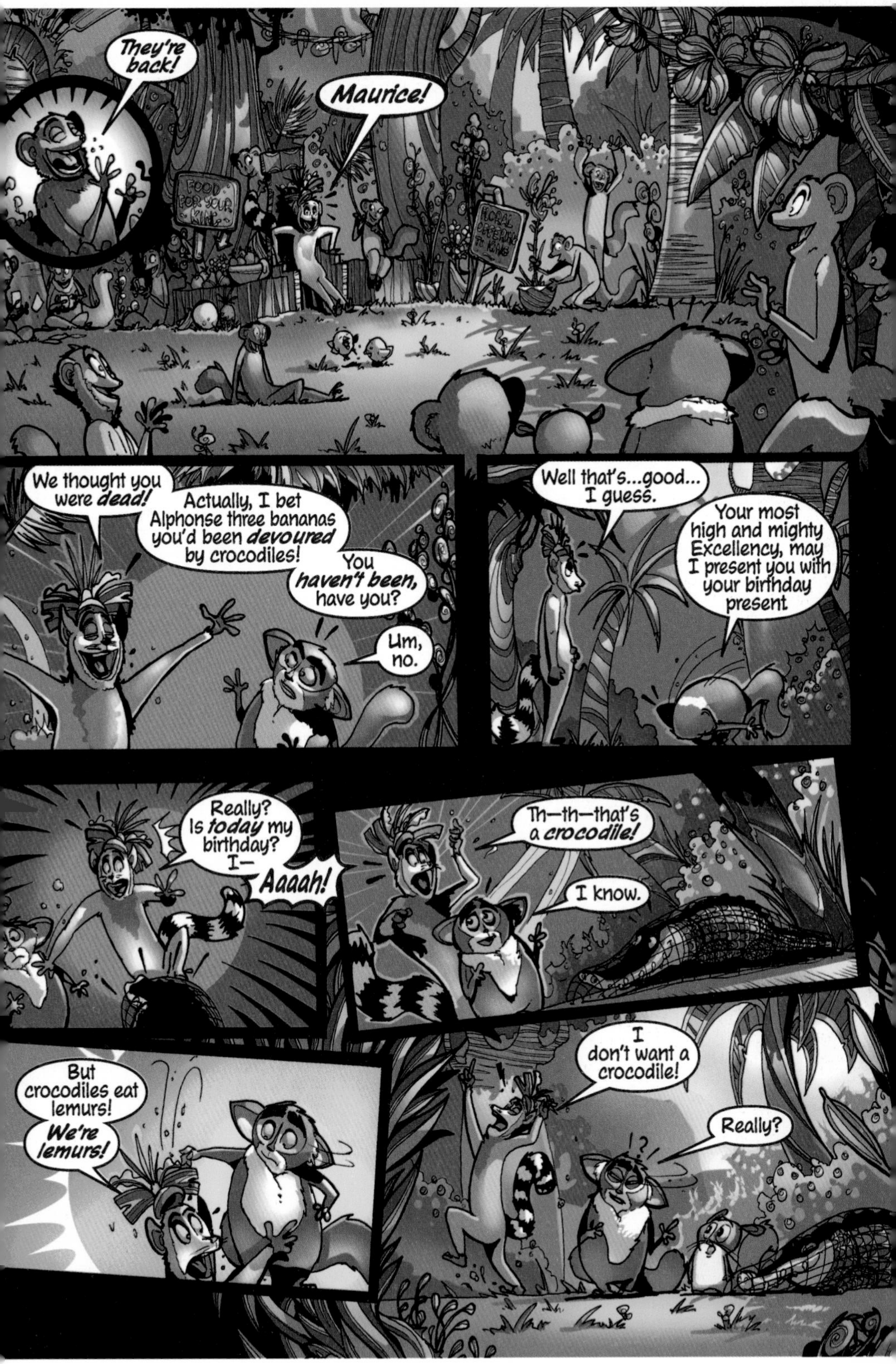
They're back!
Maurice!
We thought you were dead!
Actually, I bet Alphonse three bananas you'd been devoured by crocodiles!
You haven't been, have you?
Um, no.
Well that's...good... I guess.
Your most high and mighty Excellency, may I present you with your birthday present
Really? Is today my birthday? I—
Aaaah!
Th—th—that's a crocodile!
I know.
But crocodiles eat lemurs! We're lemurs!
I don't want a crocodile!
!?!
Really?

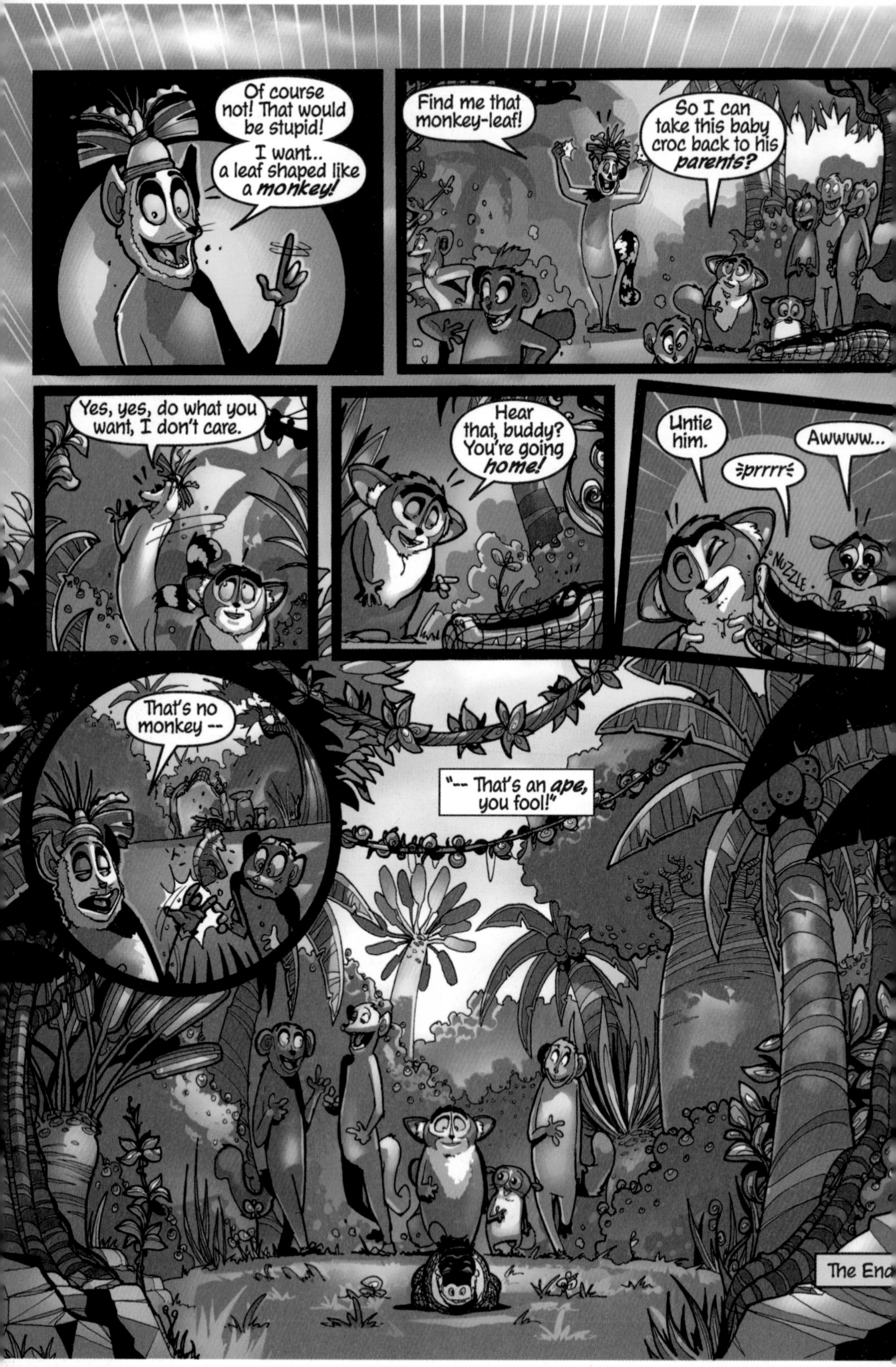

Of course not! That would be stupid!
I want.. a leaf shaped like a *monkey!*
Find me that monkey-leaf!
So I can take this baby croc back to his *parents?*
Yes, yes, do what you want, I don't care.
Hear that, buddy? You're going *home!*
Untie him.
prrrr
Awwww...
NUZZLE
That's no monkey --
"-- That's an *ape,* you fool!"
The End

OPERATION DESSERT STORM

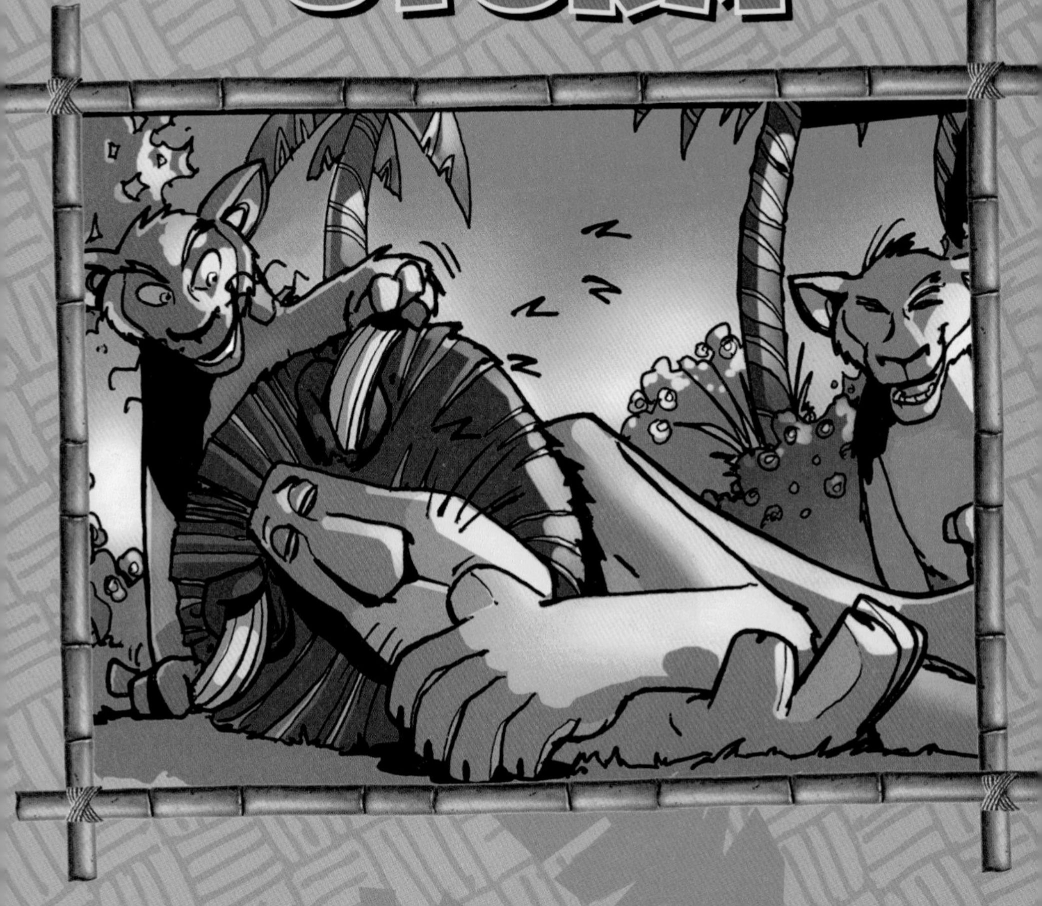

WRITER JASPRE BARK
ART LORENZO
LETTERS JIMMY BETANCOURT/COMICRAFT

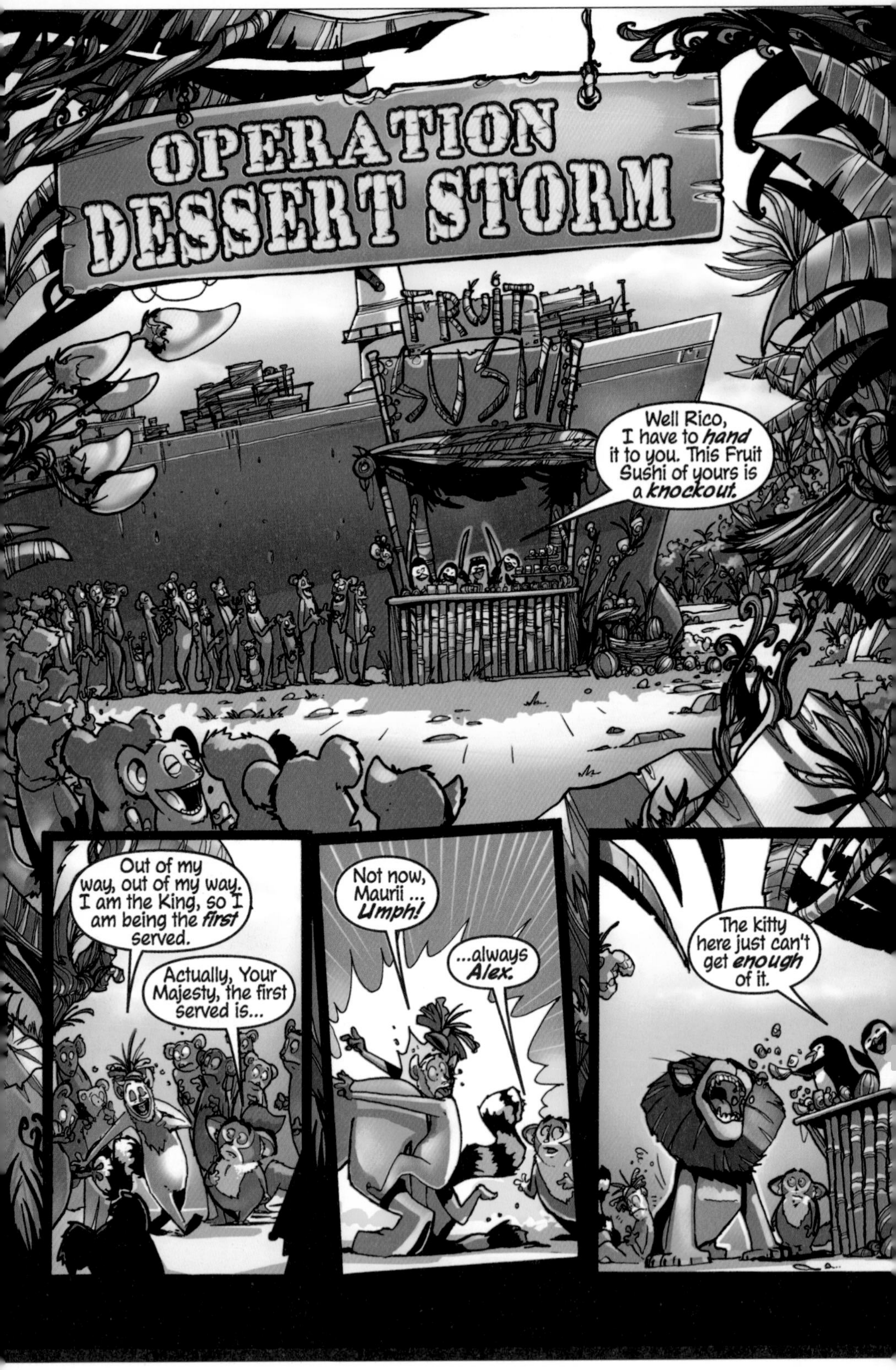
OPERATION DESSERT STORM
FRUIT SUSHI
Well Rico, I have to *hand* it to you. This Fruit Sushi of yours is a *knockout.*
Out of my way, out of my way. I am the King, so I am being the *first* served.
Actually, Your Majesty, the first served is...
Not now, Maurii ... *Umph!*
...always *Alex.*
The kitty here just can't get *enough* of it.

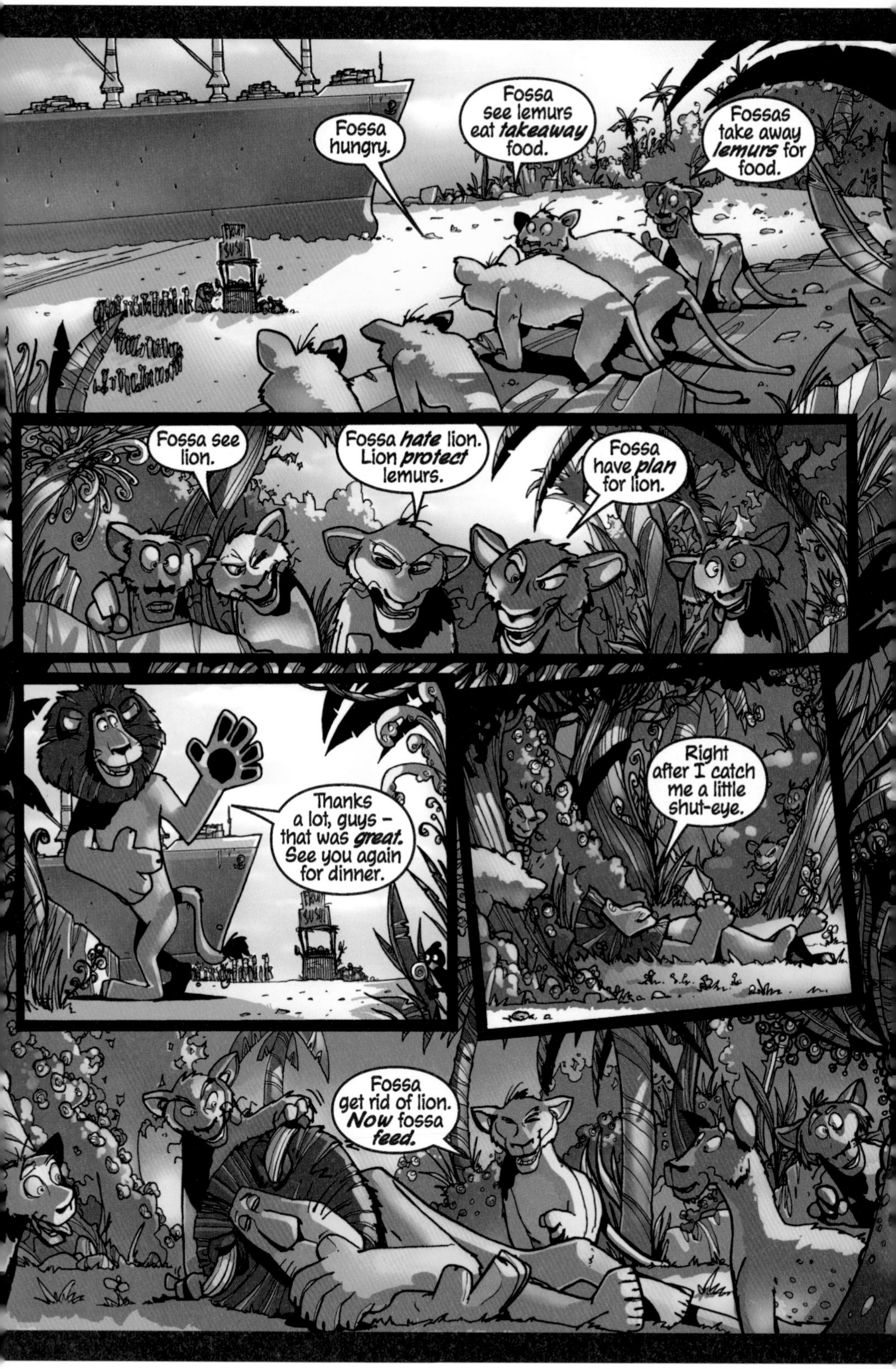

Fossa hungry.
Fossa see lemurs eat takeaway food.
Fossas take away lemurs for food.
FRUIT SUSHI
Fossa see lion.
Fossa hate lion. Lion protect lemurs.
Fossa have plan for lion.
Thanks a lot, guys – that was great. See you again for dinner.
Right after I catch me a little shut-eye.
Fossa get rid of lion. Now fossa feed.

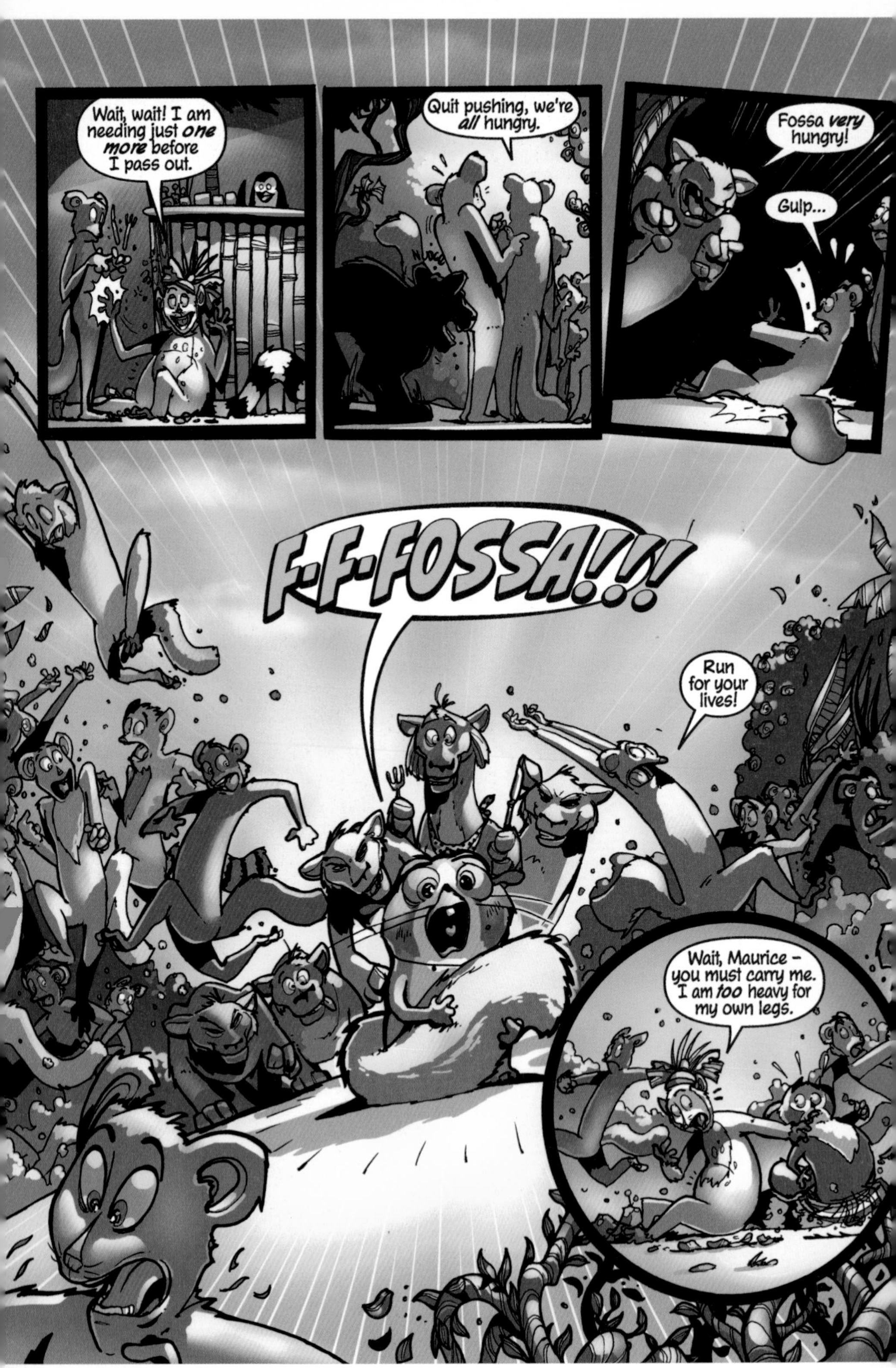
Wait, wait! I am needing just *one more* before I pass out.
Quit pushing, we're *all* hungry.
NUDGE
Fossa *very* hungry!
Gulp...
F-F-FOSSA!!!
Run for your lives!
Wait, Maurice – you must carry me. I am *too* heavy for my own legs.

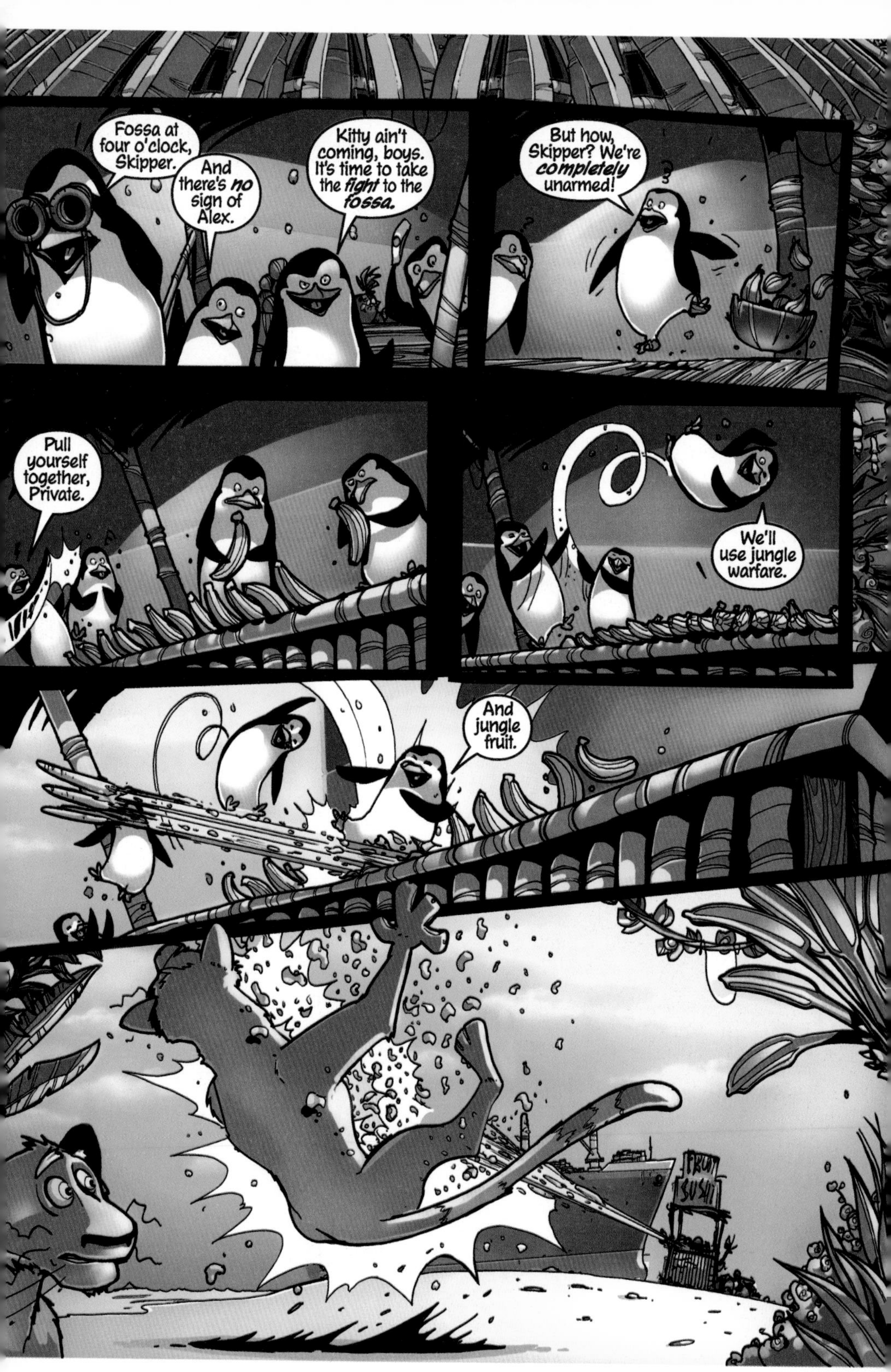

Fossa at four o'clock, Skipper.
And there's *no* sign of Alex.
Kitty ain't coming, boys. It's time to take the *fight* to the *fossa.*
But how, Skipper? We're *completely* unarmed!
Pull yourself together, Private.
We'll use jungle warfare.
And jungle fruit.
FRUIT SUSHI

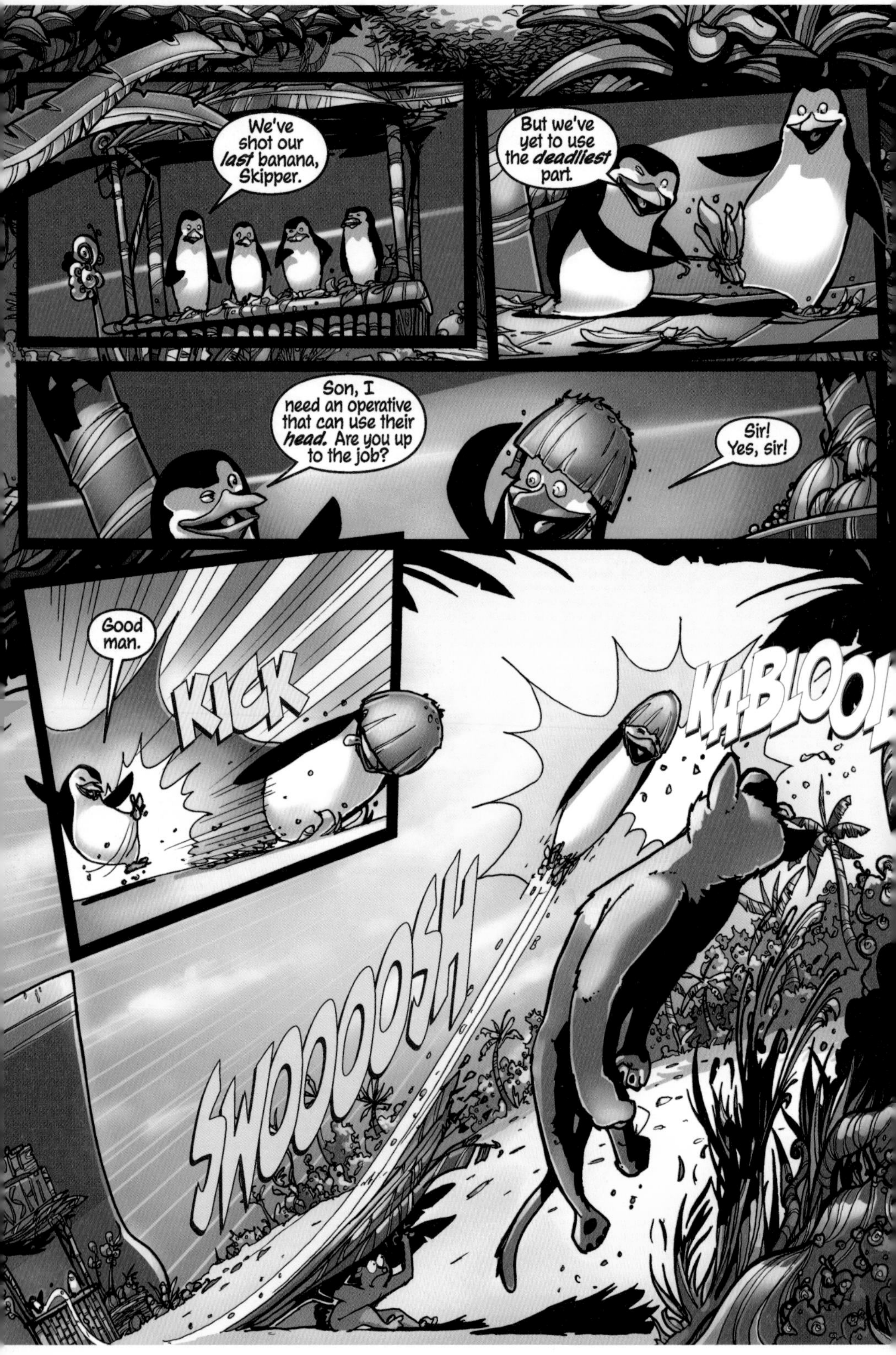

We've shot our *last* banana, Skipper.
But we've yet to use the *deadliest* part.
Son, I need an operative that can use their *head.* Are you up to the job?
Sir! Yes, sir!
Good man.
KICK
KA-BLOO
SWOOOOOSH

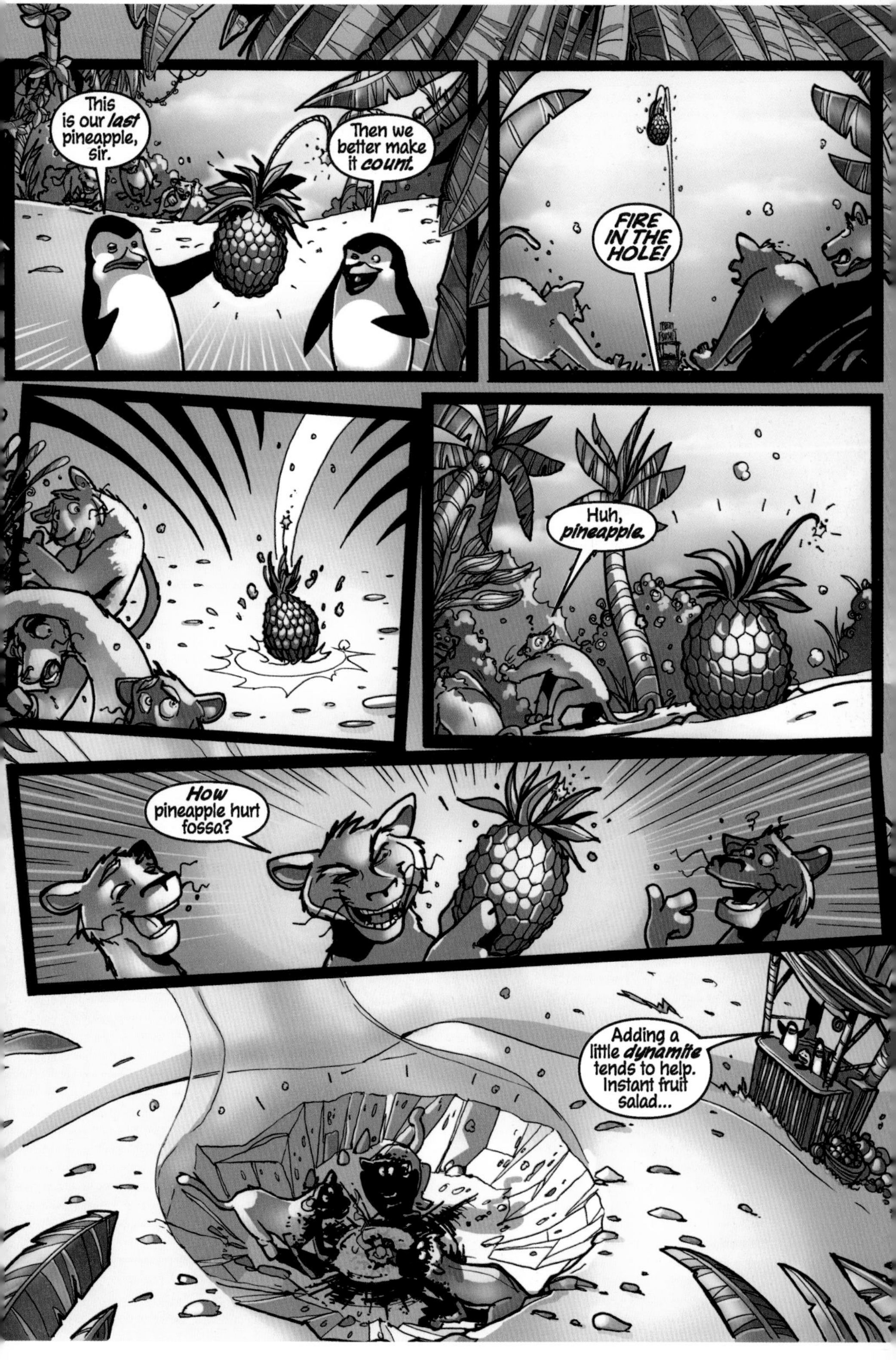
This is our *last* pineapple, sir.
Then we better make it *count.*
FIRE IN THE HOLE!
Huh, *pineapple.*
How pineapple hurt fossa?
Adding a little *dynamite* tends to help. Instant fruit salad...

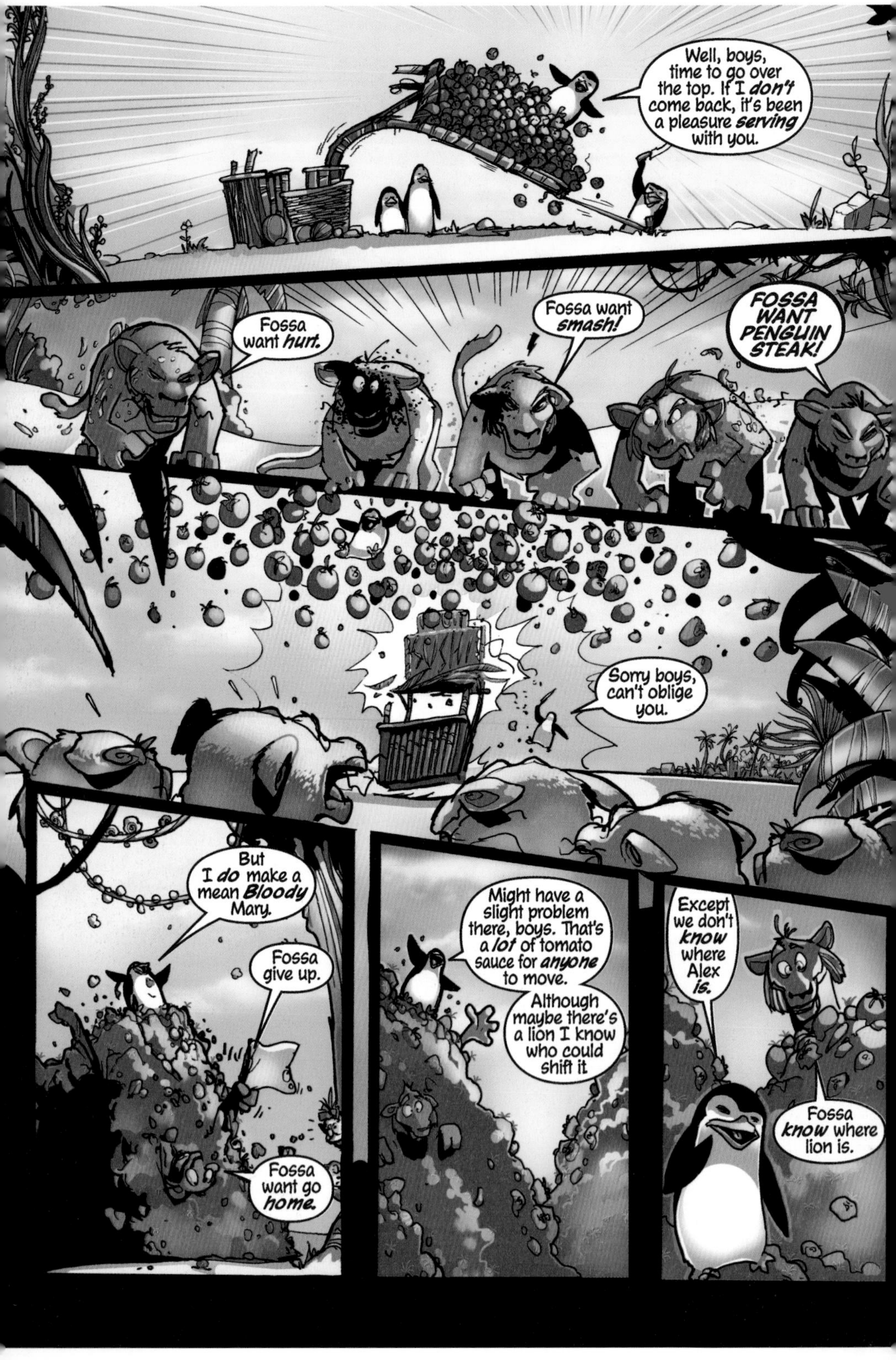
Well, boys, time to go over the top. If I *don't* come back, it's been a pleasure *serving* with you.
Fossa want *hurt.*
Fossa want *smash!*
FOSSA WANT PENGUIN STEAK!
Sorry boys, can't oblige you.
But I *do* make a mean *Bloody* Mary.
Fossa give up.
Fossa want go *home.*
Might have a slight problem there, boys. That's a *lot* of tomato sauce for *anyone* to move.
Although maybe there's a lion I know who could shift it
Except we don't *know* where Alex *is.*
Fossa *know* where lion is.

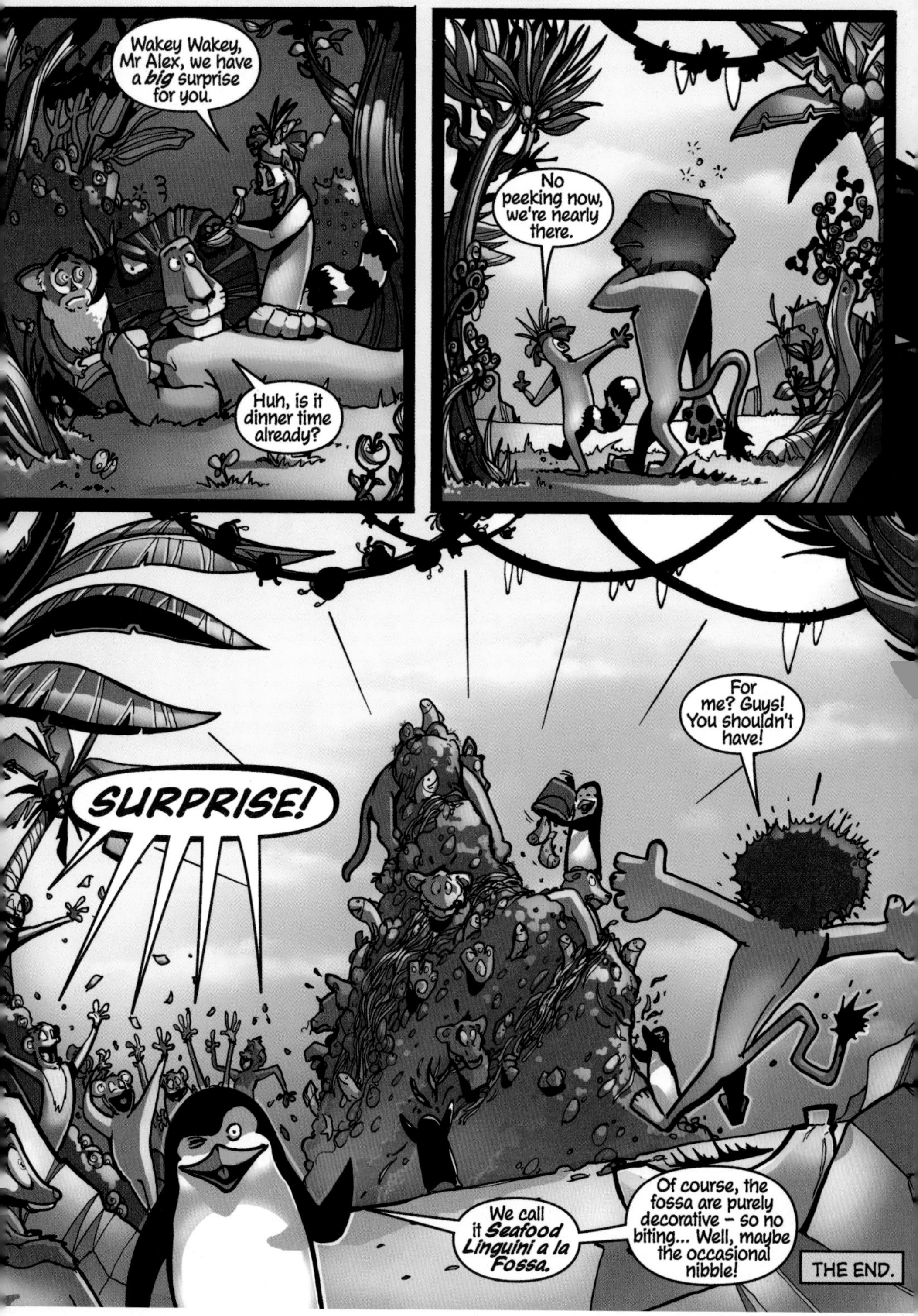
Wakey Wakey, Mr Alex, we have a *big* surprise for you.
Huh, is it dinner time already?
No peeking now, we're nearly there.
SURPRISE!
For me? Guys! You shouldn't have!
We call it *Seafood Linguini a la Fossa.*
Of course, the fossa are purely decorative – so no biting... Well, maybe the occasional nibble!
THE END.

INDEPENDENCE DAY

WRITER **JOHN GREEN**
ART **LAWRENCE ETHERINGTON**
LETTERS **JIMMY BETANCOURT/COMICRAFT**

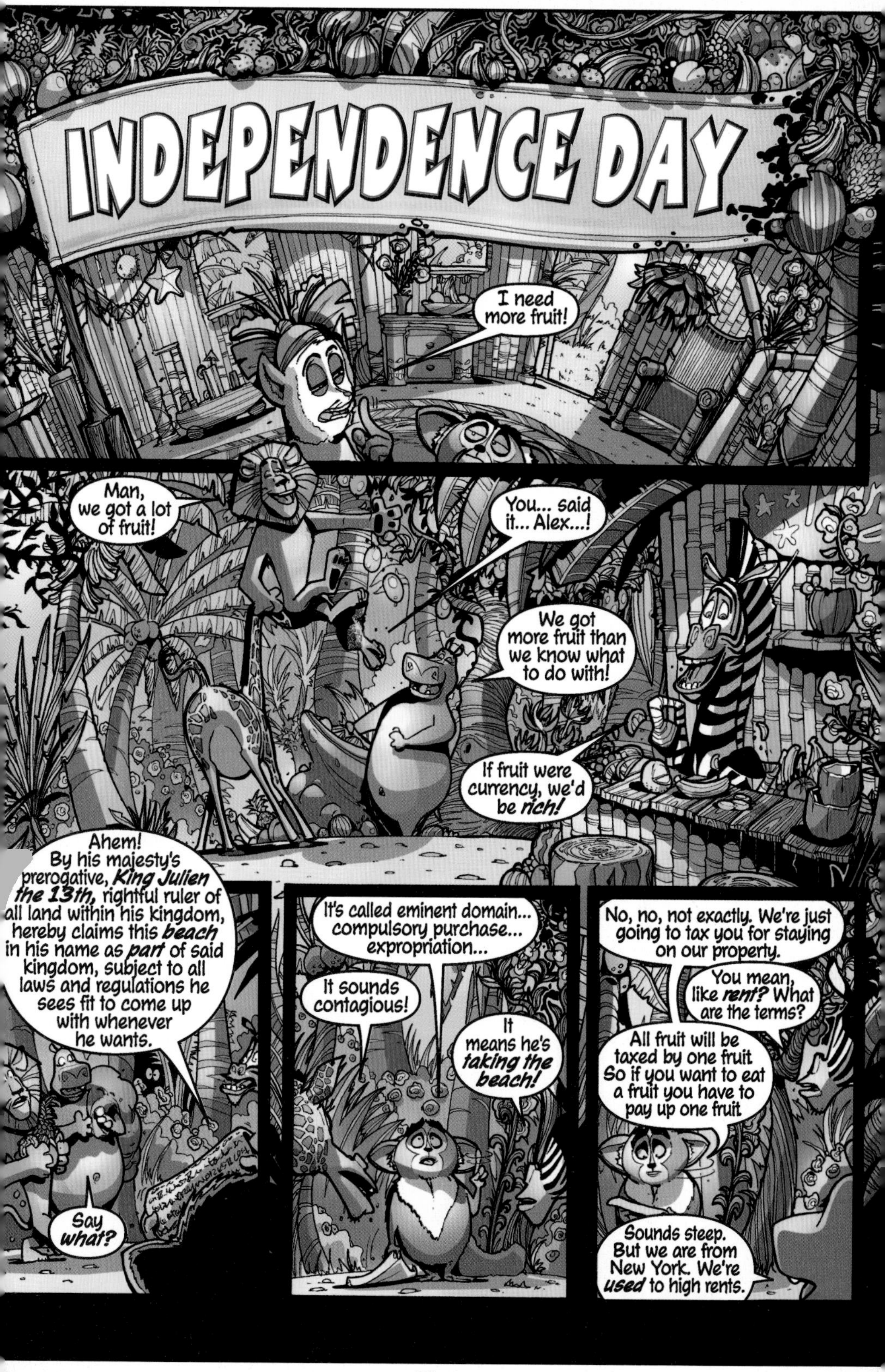
INDEPENDENCE DAY
I need more fruit!
Man, we got a lot of fruit!
You... said it... Alex...!
We got more fruit than we know what to do with!
If fruit were currency, we'd be rich!
Ahem! By his majesty's prerogative, King Julien the 13th, rightful ruler of all land within his kingdom, hereby claims this beach in his name as part of said kingdom, subject to all laws and regulations he sees fit to come up with whenever he wants.
Say what?
It's called eminent domain... compulsory purchase... expropriation...
It sounds contagious!
It means he's taking the beach!
No, no, not exactly. We're just going to tax you for staying on our property.
You mean, like rent? What are the terms?
All fruit will be taxed by one fruit So if you want to eat a fruit you have to pay up one fruit
Sounds steep. But we are from New York. We're used to high rents.

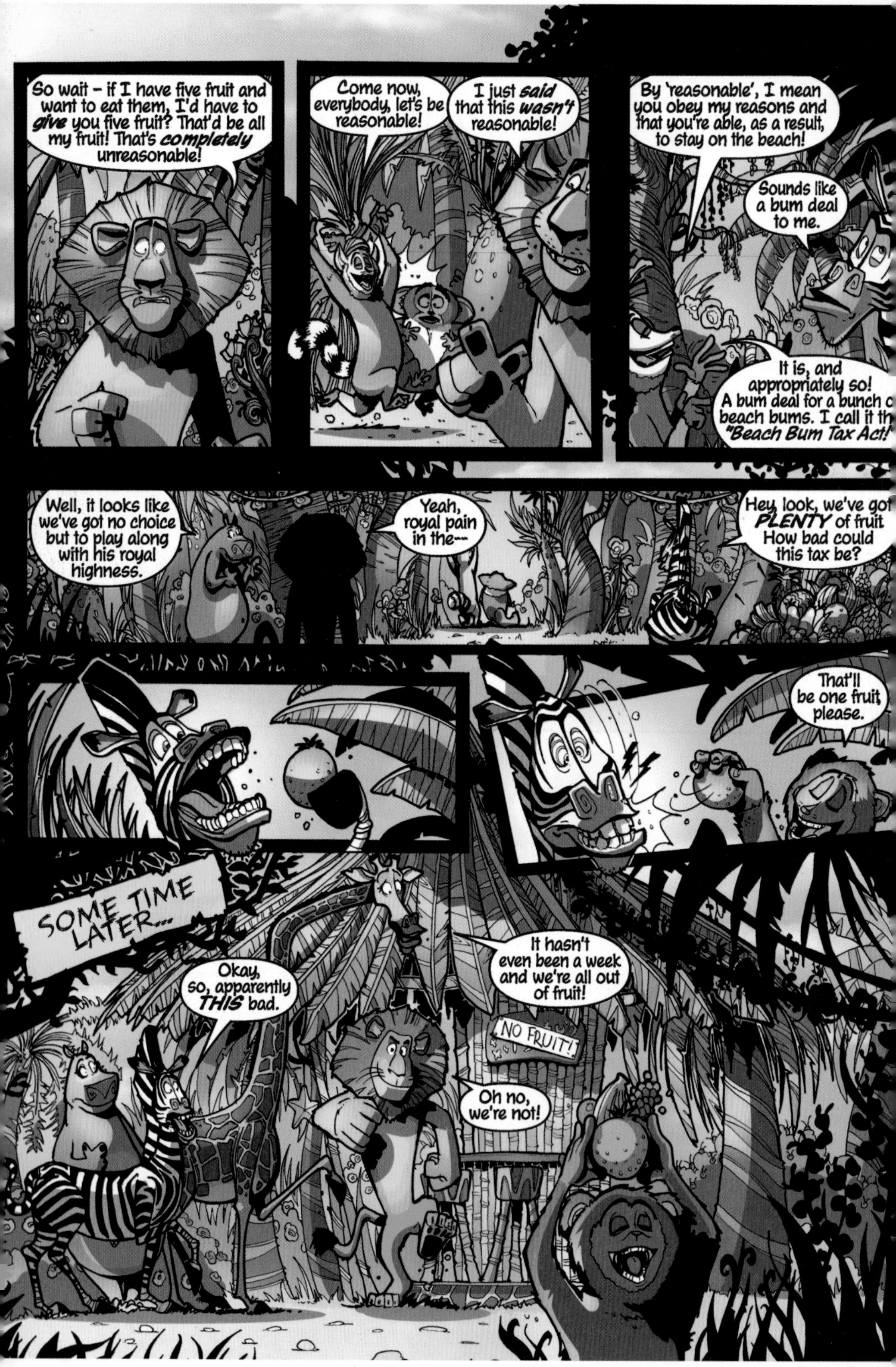
So wait – if I have five fruit and want to eat them, I'd have to *give* you five fruit? That'd be all my fruit! That's *completely* unreasonable!
Come now, everybody, let's be reasonable!
I just *said* that this *wasn't* reasonable!
By 'reasonable', I mean you obey my reasons and that you're able, as a result, to stay on the beach!
Sounds like a bum deal to me.
It is, and appropriately so! A bum deal for a bunch o
beach bums. I call it th
"Beach Bum Tax Act!
Well, it looks like we've got no choice but to play along with his royal highness.
Yeah, royal pain in the--
Hey, look, we've got *PLENTY* of fruit How bad could this tax be?
That'll be one fruit, please.
SOME TIME LATER...
Okay, so, apparently *THIS* bad.
It hasn't even been a week and we're all out of fruit!
NO FRUIT!
Oh no, we're not!

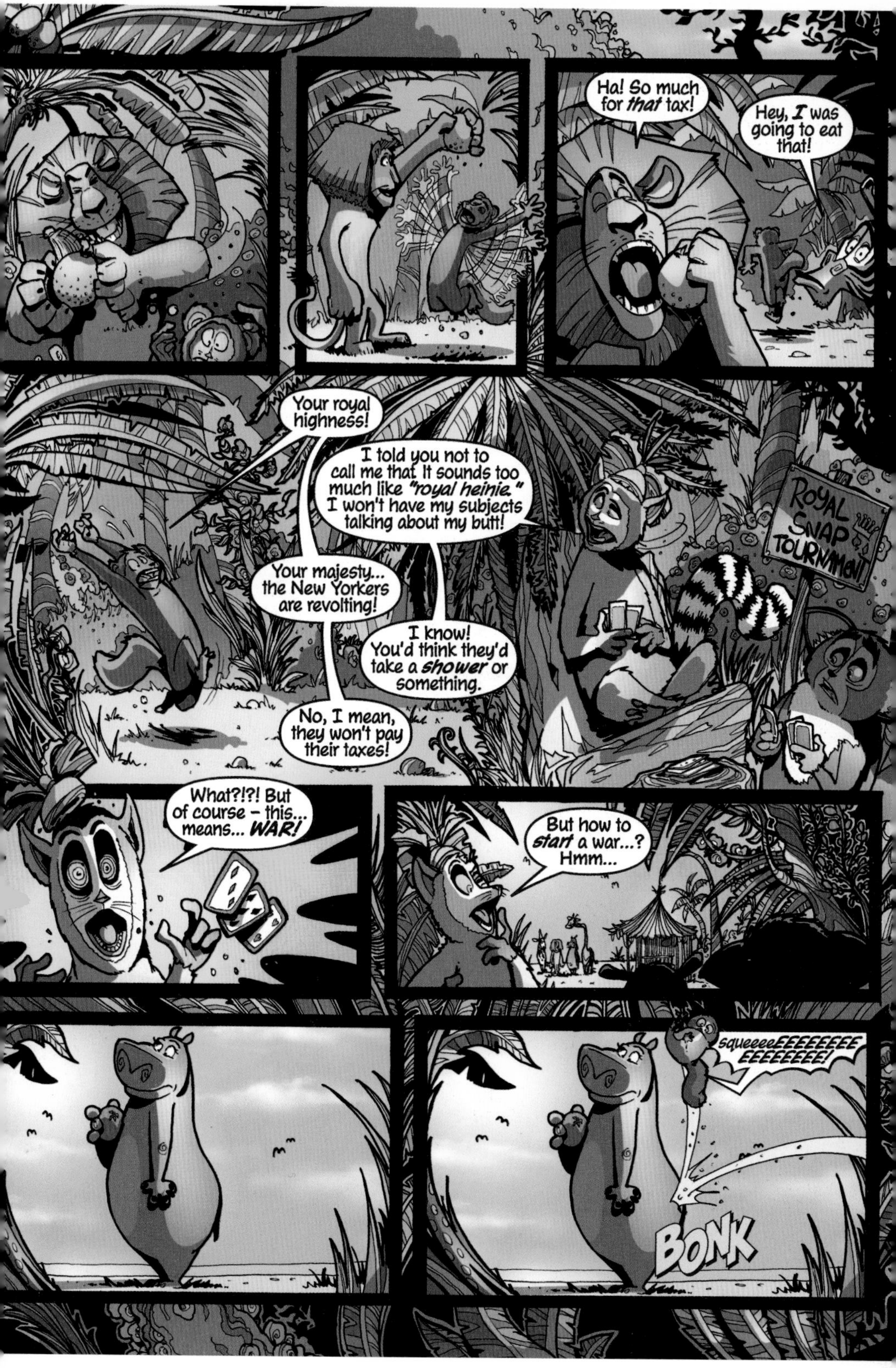
Ha! So much for *that* tax!
Hey, *I* was going to eat that!
Your royal highness!
I told you not to call me that. It sounds too much like "*royal heinie.*" I won't have my subjects talking about my butt!
Your majesty... the New Yorkers are revolting!
I know! You'd think they'd take a *shower* or something.
No, I mean, they won't pay their taxes!
ROYAL SNAP TOURNAMENT
What?!?! But of course – this... means... *WAR!*
But how to *start* a war...? Hmm...
squeeeeEEEEEEEE EEEEEEEE!
BONK

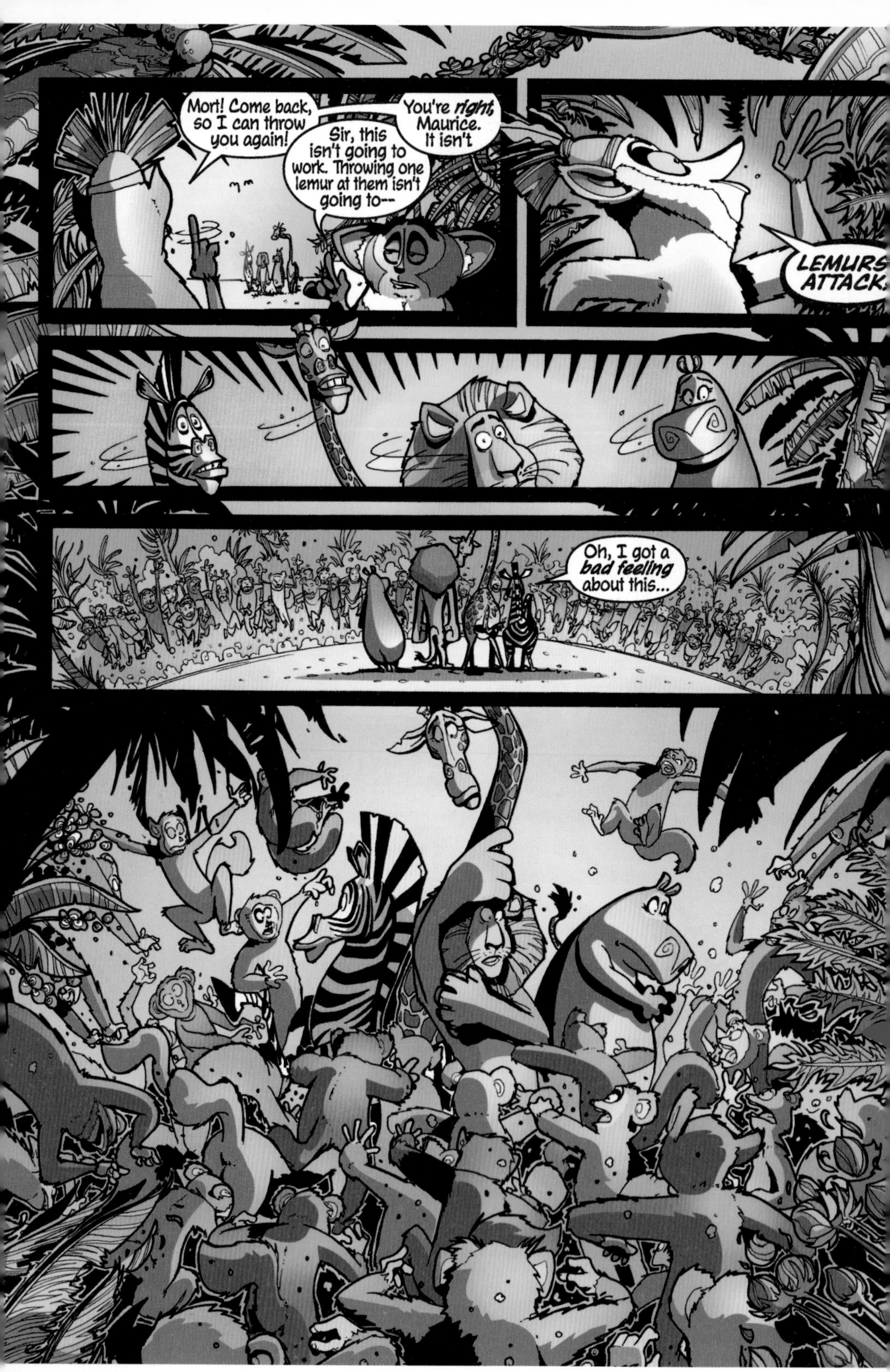

Mort! Come back, so I can throw you again!
Sir, this isn't going to work. Throwing one lemur at them isn't going to--
You're *right,* Maurice. It isn't
LEMURS ATTACK!
Oh, I got a *bad feeling* about this...

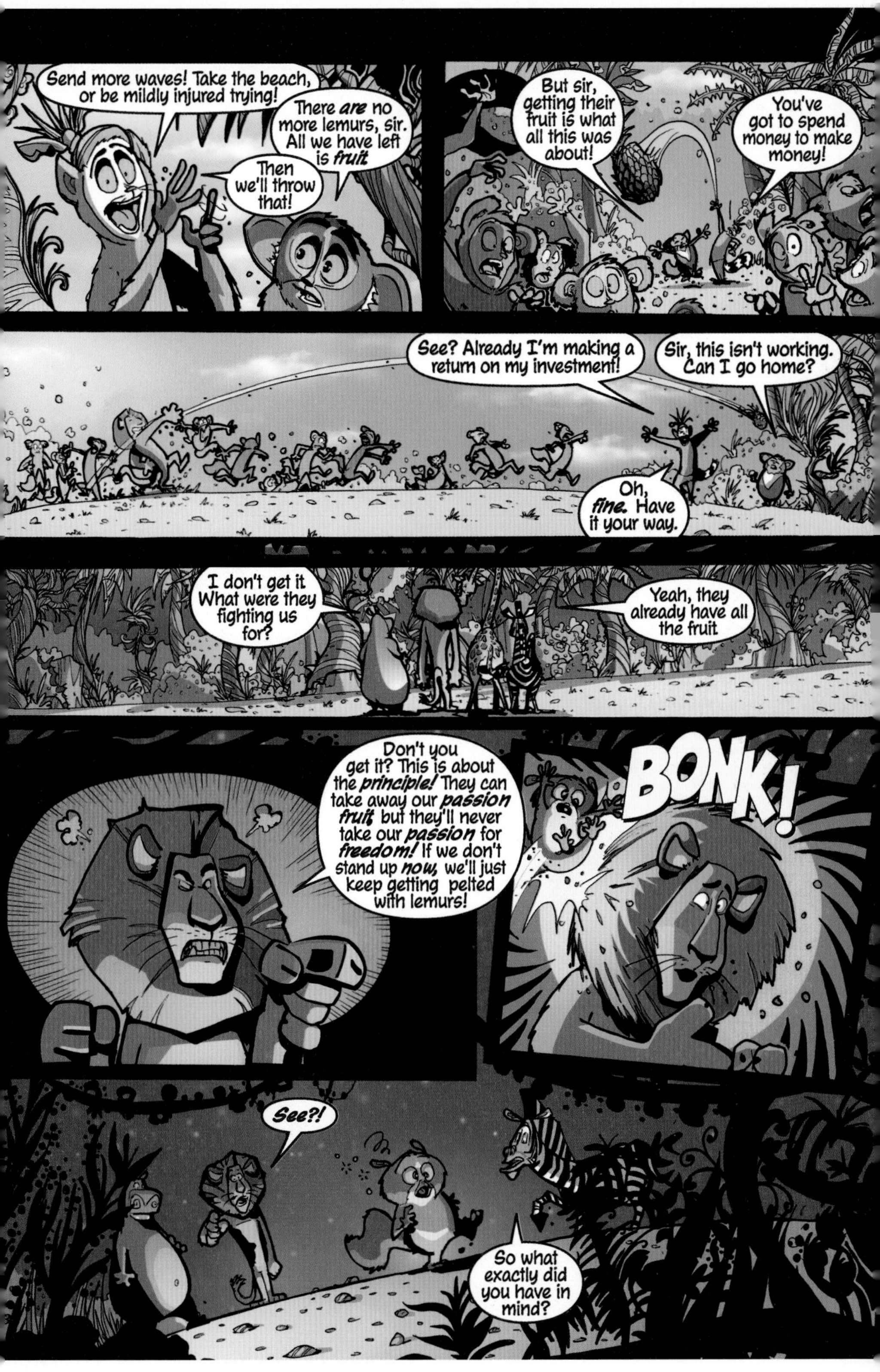

Send more waves! Take the beach, or be mildly injured trying!
There *are* no more lemurs, sir. All we have left is *fruit*
Then we'll throw that!
But sir, getting their fruit is what all this was about!
You've got to spend money to make money!
See? Already I'm making a return on my investment!
Sir, this isn't working. Can I go home?
Oh, *fine.* Have it your way.
I don't get it What were they fighting us for?
Yeah, they already have all the fruit
Don't you get it? This is about the *principle!* They can take away our *passion fruit,* but they'll never take our *passion* for *freedom!* If we don't stand up *now,* we'll just keep getting pelted with lemurs!
BONK!
See?!
So what exactly did you have in mind?

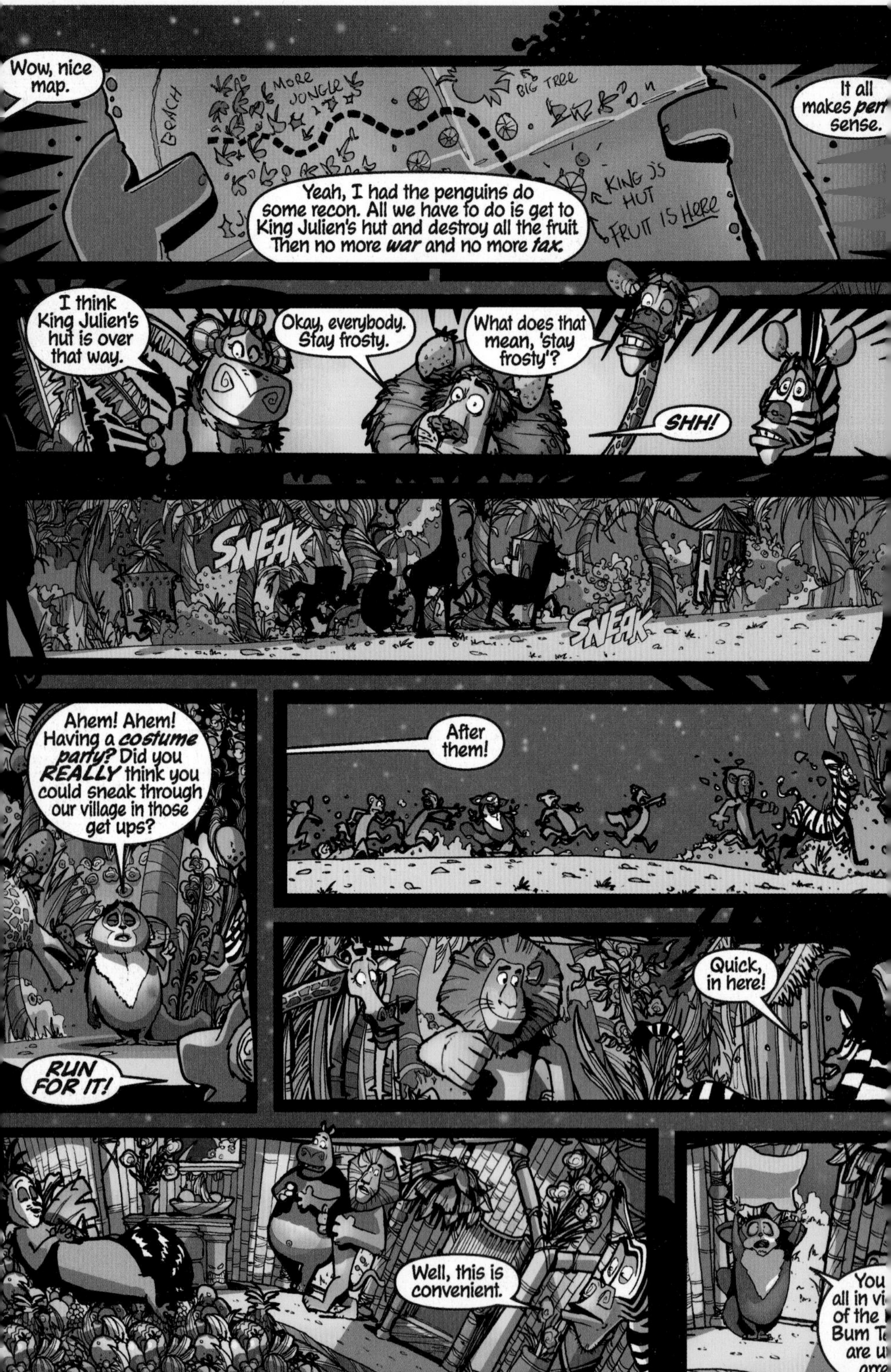
Wow, nice map.
BEACH
MORE JUNGLE
BIG TREE
KING J'S HUT
FRUIT IS HERE
Yeah, I had the penguins do some recon. All we have to do is get to King Julien's hut and destroy all the fruit Then no more war and no more tax.
It all makes per sense.
I think King Julien's hut is over that way.
Okay, everybody. Stay frosty.
What does that mean, 'stay frosty'?
SHH!
SNEAK
SNEAK
Ahem! Ahem! Having a costume party? Did you REALLY think you could sneak through our village in those get ups?
RUN FOR IT!
After them!
Quick, in here!
Well, this is convenient.
You all in vi of the Bum T are u arre

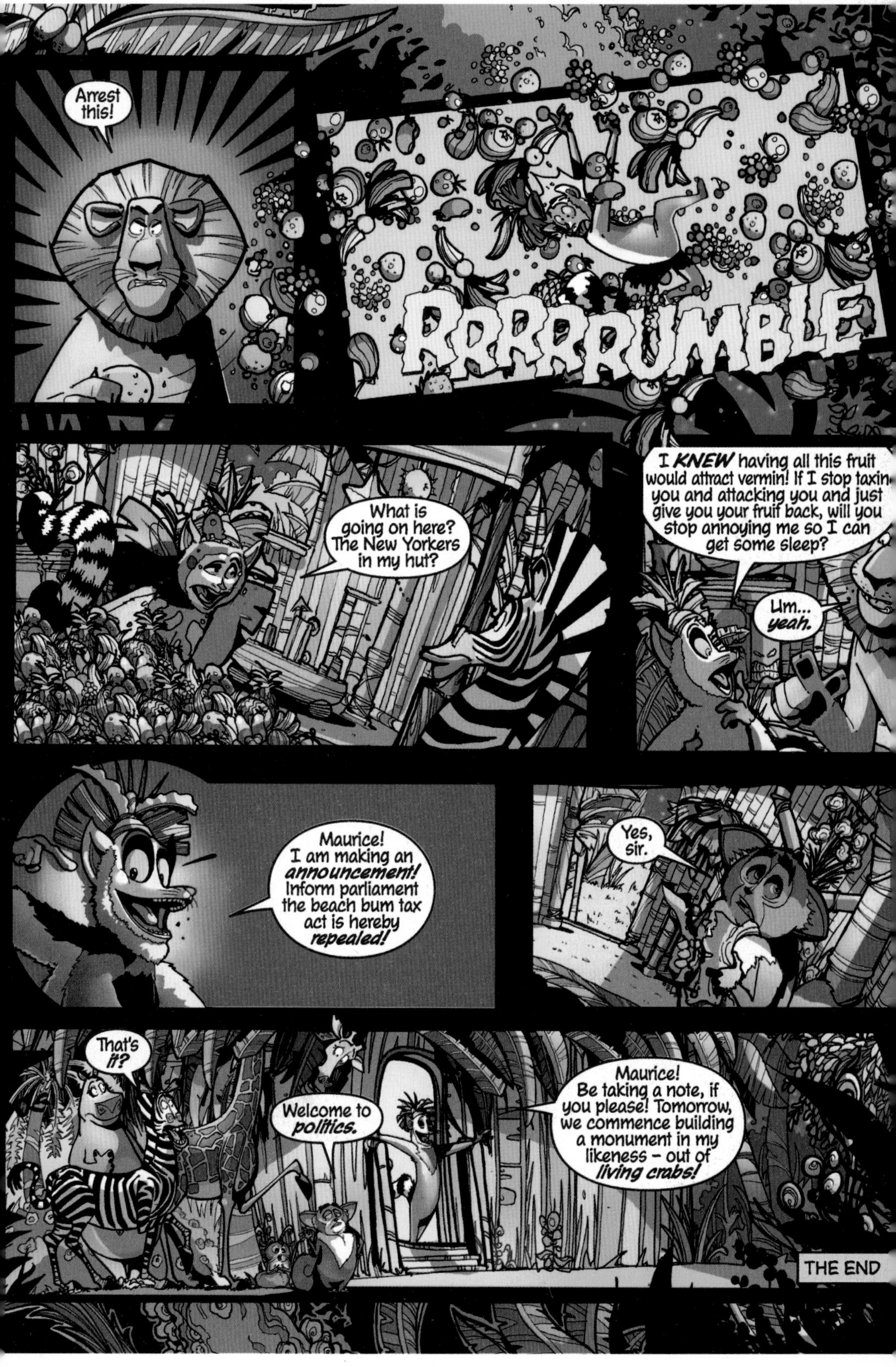

Arrest this!
RRRRRUMBLE
What is going on here? The New Yorkers in my hut?
I KNEW having all this fruit would attract vermin! If I stop taxin you and attacking you and just give you your fruit back, will you stop annoying me so I can get some sleep?
Um... yeah.
Maurice! I am making an announcement! Inform parliament the beach bum tax act is hereby repealed!
Yes, sir.
That's it?
Welcome to politics.
Maurice! Be taking a note, if you please! Tomorrow, we commence building a monument in my likeness – out of living crabs!
THE END

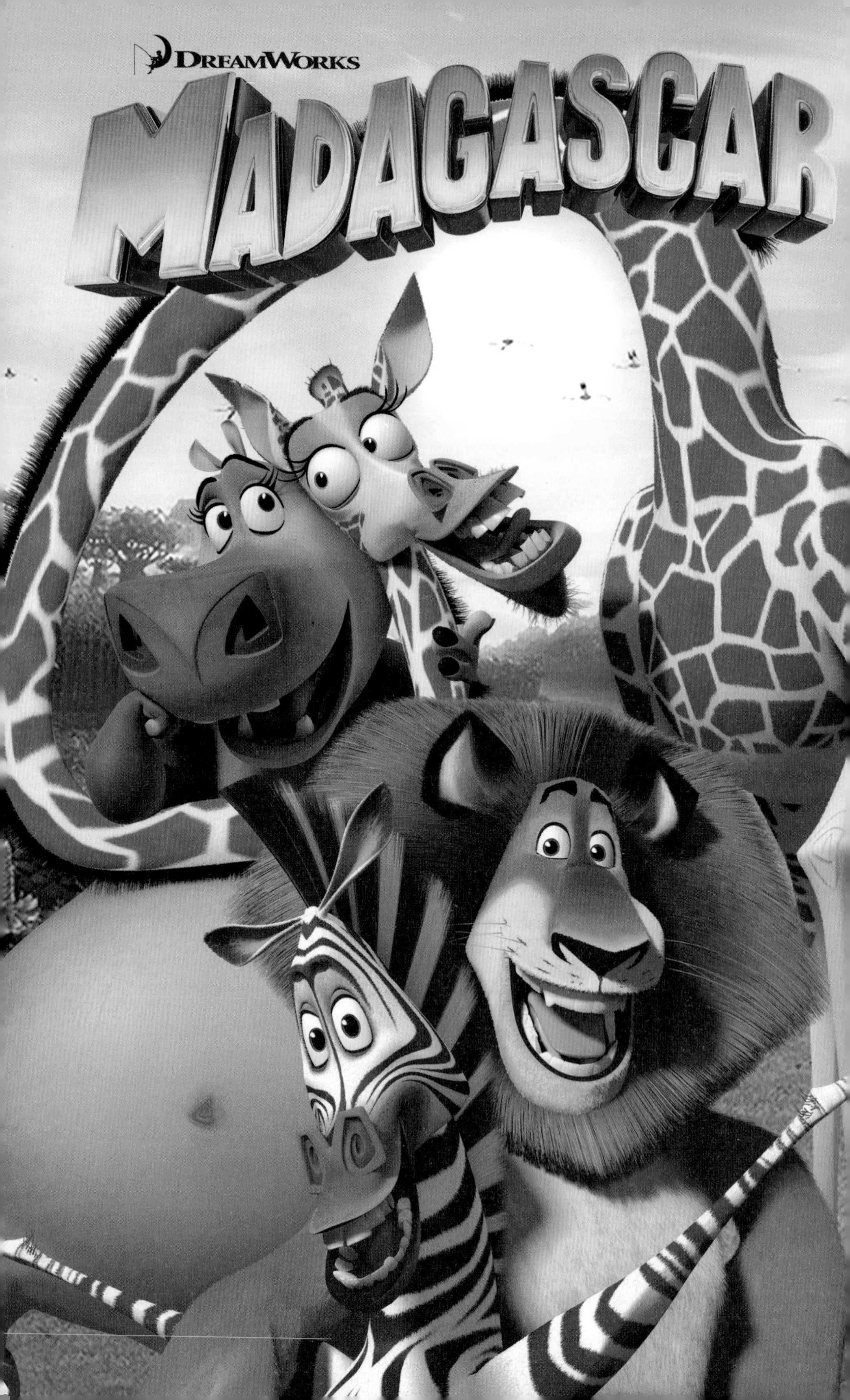
DREAMWORKS
MADAGASCAR